Jake,

Lucid Dreamer

David J. Naiman

ISBN-13: 978-84-948787-0-1

Also available as a Kindle eBook on Amazon

First Edition Kwill Books 2018

www.kwillbooks.com

For my parents (all 3)

CONTENTS

CHAPTER ONE

Few experiences are more exciting than your own dreams. Even fewer are more tiresome than listening to someone else's, but hang with me for a sec. This isn't what you think.

I wait behind the curtains of a stage next to a bunny who is juggling mice. I'm supposed to go on next, and I have absolutely no idea what I'm going to perform. Whenever I try to think up an idea, the bunny misses her catch and the mouse hits the floor, giving off a dull squeak. You can imagine how distracting this is. Then I realize that I'm practically naked. The only thing between me and total embarrassment is my flimsy underwear.

By now I should have figured out that I'm dreaming – what can be more obvious than the underwear bit? – but I don't. I'm too nervous about having to go on stage next to worry about what is and isn't normal. That's the funny thing about dreams: the ridiculous seems perfectly reasonable until the moment after you wake up.

Then it happens. I'm stressed out about my turn, clueless to the absurdity of bunnies juggling mice or, for that matter, the seagulls crossing swords with the cows or even the chimpanzees twirling in their tutus. My moment comes when the penguin tells me it's time for me to go on stage. In an absolute panic, I say no.

"No," I say.

Just to be clear, I mean that *I* say no - not the dream version of me shaking in my underwear by the stage but me, the guy in bed thinking up this nonsense for whatever reason we all dream. And when I say no, everything changes.

The dream haze lifts, and my vision becomes super clear like when I first got glasses. I move my arms and stare at my hands as though I'm an alien inhabiting a new body. And just to be clear, when I say I move my arms, I mean that *I* do this - not the dream version of me but the actual, well, you get the idea. My point is that I can control myself in the dream, and this is the coolest thing I have ever done. Ever. True, that's not saying much since I'm only a seventh grader, but it's still very cool.

I don't think the penguin agrees. He backs away and calls out for someone named Connor. A kangaroo hops over, looking none too pleased.

"You're not allowed to do that, mate," Connor says. Of course he has an Australian accent. He's a kangaroo!

"Maybe not, but I can. Check it out." I wave at him.

Connor crosses his arms. OK, how does he not get how awesome this is? I shake my whole body around, ending with wide arms and a big "Ta-da!"

The kangaroo sighs, jumps high in the air, and slams both feet directly into my face.

I wake up with a start and cuss out the kangaroo. I know quite a few cuss words thanks to middle school. My dad's not so thrilled, but I figure hey, at least I've learned something.

I pull the sheet over my head and mutter, "Connor, Connor, Connor!" to remind my brain where I left off. I've never been able to slide back into the same dream, but I try anyway. Unfortunately, if I do dream again, I don't remember it. The next thing I know, my alarm gives off an irritating buzz, and I slap the thing hard.

Groan. Another stressful day of school with all those annoying people. No wonder I only ever dream about animals.

CHAPTER TWO

On my way to the bathroom, I see Dad leaning against my sister's door. He's wearing a rumpled shirt and a distant expression, but forces a smile when he notices me.

"Good morning. Are you ready for another thrilling school day?"

I grunt.

"Yeah, I feel you."

His smile is so broad it no longer seems forced. I wish I could pull that off.

"Emma's done with the bathroom, so it's all yours," he says. "You look a bit less than excited to start your day."

That's Dad, the King of Understatement.

By the time I make it downstairs, I find Emma in front of an open cabinet, stretching for the stack of bowls. A few more inches and she's golden, but her fingertips barely brush the bottom of the pile. She flashes her cutesy look, all dimples and eyelashes, an expression that never fails to reduce Dad into a bowl of Jell-O and never fails to irritate me. I mean, come on. She'll be nine next year; she's getting way too old for the little girl act.

Oh, and she's got her stuffed monkey wrapped around her neck. Beenie. The two are inseparable. If Dad hadn't made a rule banning it, she'd take Beenie to school. Seriously. I don't know how she gets away with half the stuff she does.

I grab a bowl easily. "Did you need something?" She strains her hand higher, bouncing on her tippy toes, making an "ooo-ooo" sound as if she's the monkey instead of Beenie.

"Fine. Here." I offer her my bowl, but she ignores it.

"I want the one with Elmo."

And I want to throttle her.

"Don't you think you're kinda old for Elmo?"

"I want the one with Elmo."

"Yeah? Good luck with that."

She puts her arm down and pouts. Even Beenie glares at me.

"If you get it for me, I promise I won't wish you a happy birthday." My body flushes. I take a moment to settle down. She knows my buttons better than anybody. In fact, I think that's the definition of the word *sister*.

I get her the stupid Elmo bowl.

I realize most kids love birthdays. Who knows what's wrong with me that I don't. I vaguely remember having birthday parties when I was younger, but it's been a while. The mere thought of a birthday party throws me into a rage. I get that way sometimes. Angry, I mean. Really angry, often for reasons even I don't understand. It builds up inside me, sudden and overpowering. I do all I can just to keep it together.

"Get the spoons and milk," I say, but she's already on it.

Dad comes downstairs while I'm pouring the cereal.

"We're almost out." I hold up the box.

"Did you put it on the list?"

The list. He has a list for everything.

"No."

"How am I supposed to know to buy it if it's not on the list?"

"I'm telling you now."

"If it's not on the list, it doesn't get done."

"OK. I guess we'll have to skip breakfast and go to school hungry."

"Jake, there's other food in this house besides cereal. You're not going to starve."

His expression remains cheerful, but his irritated tone sets me off.

"Maybe, but what would Em put in her Elmo bowl?"

Dad freezes. I can tell he thinks I crossed the line. Fine, go ahead and yell at me. I don't care.

Instead, he blinks slowly.

"I'm going to let that slide since this is your special day." He walks over to the refrigerator and writes on his precious list. "Cereal. There. Now pour the milk for your sister."

Did I forget to mention this? Emma's in third grade and she can't pour her own milk.

I decide not to push it, this being my special day and all.

After I scarf down my cereal, I plant myself in front of the TV for morning cartoons. In the background, I can hear Dad getting Emma ready for school. He drops her off on his way to work at Before Care and trusts me to lock up on my way to the bus stop. Being the big brother does have its advantages.

Dad sits next to me on the couch. "Pause, please."

I hit the remote.

"I'll ask this only once, I promise. Are you sure you don't want to do anything for your birthday?"

"I'm sure."

"OK. I'll bring home your favorite for dinner, we'll do gifts, and that will be the end of it. You're going to like your present from Mom and me."

I shoot him a look. This time he's the one who's crossed the line.

"Mom? Is this a sick joke?"

"She and I had talked about this before...you know."

"Before she died?"

"Yes, Jake. Before she died."

7

He tries to put his arm around me. I pull away.

"Are you going to be all right today?"

"What am I going to do? Cry?"

"It would be OK if you did."

OK with him maybe. I'm not OK with that.

"I'm fine. Can I watch the rest of this?"

He kisses my head before I can react.

"Happy birthday, Jake."

CHAPTER THREE

My school bus pulls up to the entrance. Huge block letters over the doors spell out Pine Woods Middle School, but don't let the name fool you. The building is in a clearing with only a few spindly trees sprouting up along the sidewalk. I think the school system picks the name based on whatever they have to chop down in order to put up the building. My last school was named Mighty Oak Elementary. That must have been one heck of a tree.

When I get to my locker, I scout the area. Now that I'm in seventh grade, I only have to deal with eighth graders slapping the books out of my hands. My odds of being humiliated have dropped in half from last year. Look at me being all optimistic. Dad would be proud.

The coast is clear except for Will, whose locker is next to mine. I'm not worried about him. Will's the new kid, tall and kinda quiet. I heard he was a surfer from California. That's the rumor anyway. It could be true. He wears colorful shirts, sports a tan, and has long, blond hair. Maybe he had friends at his old school, but he doesn't fit in too well around here. We don't meet a lot of surfer dudes in Maryland.

"What's up?" Will says.

I respond with a curt nod while I gather my books for the sprint to homeroom. I suppose I could be friendlier, but who knows if Will even wants to be my friend. He's probably being nice to everyone until he figures out who the cool kids are. I'm just sparing him the disappointment. In case it isn't obvious, I'm not one of the cool kids.

Middle school blows. I would never say this out loud, but I miss elementary school. Yeah, it was lame, but at least things were simpler.

Here's how I see it: In the educational family, elementary school is the baby sister with her button nose and rosy cheeks. She parades in her oh-so-cute Halloween costume, squeaks out her first notes in band, and has her scribbles posted on the refrigerator for all the world to gush and rave about.

At the other extreme is the big brother, high school. He's practically an adult, with his driver's permit, growth spurt, and college applications. He glows with potential.

Lost in between is middle school, the forgotten child, awkward and pimply. That's where I am, surrounded by braces, gangly limbs, sour attitudes, and raging hormones.

I slam my locker shut. Sure, nothing bad has happened today, but it's still early. Give it time.

We don't change classrooms between homeroom and mod one, so when the bell rings, my science teacher starts class right away. Mrs. Vespa wears huge metal bracelets on both wrists so every time she moves, she sounds like a wind chime. You can hear her coming clear down the hallway. That constant clanging would drive me nuts, but she seems to enjoy it. I think she swings her arms sometimes just to hear the music.

She's teaching an environmental science unit, focusing on the many ways people alter the environment. You know, overpopulation, habitat destruction, climate change, pollution, that sort of thing. Not exactly uplifting stuff. This is, by far, my favorite class this year.

Mrs. Vespa clasps her hands together. *Jangle, jangle.* "I have exciting news. We're going to do group mini projects and present them to the class on Monday."

The class groans. Today is Thursday. There goes the weekend.

"Now, now. Everybody calm down. This'll be low-key and fun. We'll break into groups of three."

That leads to another commotion. Friends signal each other. Within seconds, the class has fragmented. The four girls in the back start bickering. Already, one is in tears.

"Quiet please. Let me finish." Mrs. Vespa flaps her arms furiously, but few people pay her any attention. We've learned to tune out her wrist chimes. She raises her voice. "I've already picked ten group leaders based on your grades from the last exam. If you don't like it, study harder next time." That silences the class. "The leaders will choose two people with whom they wish to work. I will assign a group to anyone not picked by tomorrow. OK?" She motions to the girls in the back. "And I think you four need to split up."

Now they're all pouting.

"I'm going to call the leaders up one by one to discuss the projects. You'll address a global concern. The assignment will be to find ways in which we can affect positive change. For now, everybody get out the worksheet we began yesterday and work quietly.

"Norman." The usual titters follow. Norman is the one kid in the class lower on the social pecking order than me. He's actually a really smart guy; it's a shame he has no social skills. I feel sorry for whoever gets put in his group – probably whoever else in this class has no friends. Oh, right. That would be me.

"Aiden." His name also provokes a reaction but only because it's unexpected. Not by me though. I used to be friends with Aiden. I know he's way smarter than he pretends to be. Aiden obsesses over his social standing even more than I do. And unlike me, he'll do whatever he thinks he must to stay ahead.

"Jessica." Jess. She and I were friendly during the early years at Mighty Oak Elementary. We haven't talked much since. When she came up to me on the first day of class to say hello, I hardly recognized her. She's – how should I put this? – more developed than I remember her. And more stylish. We've only had four weeks of school so far and she's already on her third hairstyle. Right now, it's in crazy-tight braids. That must have taken hours. I try not to stare.

I just wish I knew what to say to her. Jess and I used to talk all the time. We'd swap stories about how our white dads interact with their in-laws. That's always good material for a laugh. Her mom's black and mine's Chinese. *Was* Chinese. I'm supposed to use the past tense since she's dead and all. I don't really get that. I mean, is she no longer

Chinese because she's dead? It doesn't seem like dying should change your race. I don't know. Whatever. Thinking about Mom makes me sad. "What's the matter, Jake? Worried you'll be in Norman's group?"

I turn to find Nick, the biggest jerk to roam the earth since the rise of the hyenas. His face is all scrunched up like he's sucking on a lemon. I don't know if he has anything in his mouth, but I can say for sure that he sucks. Strangely enough, until third grade, me, Nick, and Aiden hung out all the time. We shared everything, including our secrets. Nick would later use those secrets as weapons to embarrass Aiden and me.

Aiden was more upset about Nick's betrayal than I was, yet Aiden was the one to make up with him. I guess he figured it'd be better for his social standing. Aiden and I didn't hang out so often after that. We never had a fight or anything; we just drifted apart. That was third grade, four years ago, the year Mom died. Things have been generally terrible ever since. "You know what group I mean." Nick says this loudly to be sure he has an audience. "The loser group."

I almost think Nick hates me more *because* we used to be friends. I wish he'd ignore me like I try to ignore him. No such luck. Nick has never stopped picking at the scab of our old friendship.

Norman hovers over his worksheet as if it's so fascinating he couldn't possibly hear Nick insulting him from two seats away. I call this the ostrich technique. I don't know how well sticking your head in the sand works for ostriches, but in middle school, it's a fail. Lucky for Norman, he's not the target right now. That'd be me. "You'd be perfect for the loser group, Jake. I can tell from looking at you. You know, if it walks like a duck and talks like a duck, then it's a duck." Nick laughs as though he's said something witty and glances behind him to make sure the four girls in the back are listening.

Unfortunately, they are. I mentally prepare myself the onslaught of abuse. But before Nick can open his mouth again, Will spins around. "Ducks don't talk." That's what he says. The guy hasn't spoken in class all year before this. We all just stare at him. "Ducks don't talk," he says. "The expression is 'If it walks like a duck and *quacks* like a duck, then it's probably a duck.' Ducks don't talk. And if you actually knew what a loser looked like, you'd see one every time you looked in a mirror."

Oh, snap. The girls in the back burst out giggling. Nick fumes. He's better at dishing it out than taking it and his attempt at a comeback is a mess. "Yeah, well...you...I mean, that..."

"Hey, Will." I hike my thumb at Nick. "If it sputters like a duck..."

When Will laughs, his hair whips around his face. Nick kicks Will's desk. "If it kicks like a duck," Will says. Nick hyperventilates. I think his head might explode. Hey, that's a good one.

"If his head explodes like a duck."

Will nods furiously. His hair is one blond blur. "Nice one, brah."

"Bra?" Nick's eyes flash. "He's your bra? Do you two, like, wear each other like girl's underwear?" The giggles in the back shift in Nick's favor. Will appears stunned by the comment. I'm not. If you back a rat into a corner, it'll show its true nature every time.

"Do you two hold hands and skip around? Tra-la-la-la."

Over the summer, Dad took Em and me to our first gay wedding. Two of his college friends tied the knot. I was all nervous when we got there, but it turned out to be like every other wedding I've been dragged to. Except for the two dudes part. But even that wasn't a big deal after a while. I wish Nick had been there. Then maybe he would realize what an absolute ass he was being.

"Do you, like, wear high heels and dresses?"

I nudge Will. "If it's ignorant like a duck."

That finally shuts Nick up. For now.

CHAPTER FOUR

The moment class ends, I hustle around to the door so I can catch Aiden before he leaves. Success.

"Oh hey, Aiden. Have you picked out your group yet?"

Aiden sighs. Someone with more self-esteem would have found that insulting. "No, why?" He gives me a blank look. Seriously? He's going to make me say it?

"You know, we work well together. I mean, we have in the past." Still the blank look.

"Can I be in your group?" He scans the room, probably calculating the hit his social status will take by associating with me so publicly. "Come on," I say. "You know I'll pull my weight."

"Fine, but I get to pick the third person."

"Yeah, of course."

"Oh. I thought you'd want Will in the group." Now it's my turn for the blank look.

"OK," he says. "That's all right. I just don't want Will in my group. He's a freak."

"What? No, he's not."

"Well, he talks weird."

I shake my head. "Don't be like Nick."

If there's one thing Aiden and I still agree on, it's that being like Nick is the worst possible thing a person can do. "I'm not being like Nick; I just don't want Will around. Do you want to be in my group or not?"

"Forget it. I'll find another group." Aiden takes a step back and I notice Jess staring at us. I don't know how long she's been there. When she sees me notice her, she scrambles past.

"You'll probably get stuck with Norman, you know." His tone is almost apologetic.

"Maybe. I don't care."

"Fine, you can be in my group. Don't be such a baby."

I finally get what I want, and now I don't want it anymore. "I said, forget it."

"Whatever." Aiden brushes past me. Then he spins back around. "Nick may be a jerk, but he's right about you. I pretend not to see it since we used to be friends, but you've become real moody since your mother died."

My face flushes. A tightness strangles my chest and throat. I can barely get two words out.

"Screw you!"

Those are the two words. This about sums up my relationship with most people.

Today's a B day, so mod four is gym. Except for one girl who skipped a grade, I'm the youngest person in my class. I missed the deadline for kindergarten by a month, but I think I knew all my letters or something, so they let me in anyway. My pediatrician tells me I'm at a normal height for my age, not that it matters. I'm a shrimp compared to most of my class.

We're told to pair up and practice bumping a volleyball. Will comes right over. I hadn't even noticed he was in my gym class before today. "Are you any good?" he asks.

"Not really."

"That's all right. I'll give you some pointers."

"I thought you were a surfer."

Will smiles. "I've surfed a few times, but beach volleyball is more my thing." He sets the ball to himself five times in a row. Each time, the ball settles perfectly between his fingertips. The guy's a ringer.

"Cool. The one thing I like about volleyball is spiking, only I can never get a good set." I cringe inwardly the moment I tell him that. Obviously, the real problem is my height.

"Great. I'll set it and you spike it at me."

I fix my glasses. I tend to do that when I don't know what to say.

"Seriously. Aim right below my chest." Will pats the target. "Hard as you can."

He sets the ball with perfect placement. I hit it gently anyway. He bumps the ball and catches it.

"I know you can hit harder than that. Come on, brah."

"Please don't call me 'bra.'"

"Not bra, *brah*."

I shrug.

"It means bro."

"Say 'bro' then, don't say 'bra.'"

"Not bra, *brah*."

"Yeah, I'm still not hearing a difference."

He mumbles something that sounds like a cuss word and then *Maryland*. "Just spike the ball as hard as you can," he says.

We try again. As requested, I use my full force. He bumps it back for another perfectly placed set. "Good. Spike it again."

I get in two more shots before my aim goes wide. He chases after the ball. By this time, we have spectators. "All right. Three in a row is pretty good. Let's try for ten."

"You seriously want me to spike the ball at you as hard as I can, ten times in a row?"

"Yeah, br- Jake. Let's do this."

Mr. C. peeks over the crowd. I don't think my gym teacher even knows my name. To be fair, I don't know his name either, but that's because he told us to call him Mr. C. I think the C stands for Czajkawtzyk or something. Even the other teachers call him Mr. C.

Will sets the ball, and I start wailing on it. The crowd counts each spike. My fourth hit goes wide, but Will stretches for it. He and I shift together to keep the rally going.

The crowd tracks us. "Five...six...seven."

My arm aches but if Will can take it, I'm not going to quit. Number eight veers to the side. Somehow, he still gets to it. "Two more!"

Number nine's a bit low, and Will stumbles to dig it up. I race backwards to get under number ten. I'm off balance, but I figure if I can spike it in his general direction, he'll get a piece of it. I reach back and slam the volleyball as hard as I can.

I really don't see everything that happens next. After righting myself, I find Will holding his arms out to the side. At the same moment I realize the ball is nowhere near him, I hear a horrible slapping sound. The crowd gasps. Brandon, the tallest, meanest, scariest seventh-grader on the entire eastern seaboard, rises to his feet and rubs his cheek.

"Who did that?" he says in his deep voice. Compared with him, I sing soprano.

The crowd parts and turns to me. Brandon's glare follows their direction. He looks around again and back at me, clearly not convinced I could be responsible. "Sorry, Brandon," I say. I raise my hand like a pro. "I lost my balance and my spike went wide. Totally my bad."

I might as well reason with a grizzly bear. Brandon charges straight at me, jaw clenched, fists up. I race through the crowd, zigzagging, juking the way I play Madden, doing whatever I can to keep as many people between me and Brandon as possible. I wish I was in one of my dreams so I could wake myself up and end this.

Mr. C. blows his whistle. He jogs over to Brandon and talks into his ear. They're practically the same height. My gym teacher calls me over. I stand next to these two giants and agree with whatever Mr. C. says until Brandon calms down.

What a relief! I don't even want to consider how a

fight between me and Brandon would end. Actually, there's not much to consider. I'd wind up in a hospital or a morgue, and he'd be in police custody. Good thing Mr. C. saw everything. I'm almost sorry that I make fun of his mustache.

OK, so here's the thing about Mr. C. He carries two accessories with him at all times: a whistle on a string around his neck, and a mustache comb in his shirt pocket. Seriously, he has a mustache comb. I've seen him use it sometimes when he thinks no one is watching. He strokes that huge caterpillar on his upper lip five times on each side and twice in the center. Yes, I counted. Every time is the same. Five, five, two. Five, five, two. "Are we good here? Am I going to have any problems with you guys?"

"No," I say.

Brandon grunts.

"Good. Now shake hands like men."

I put my hand out and Brandon slaps it. I'm pretty sure it's not an angry slap but more of an I-can't-be-bothered kinda thing. I hope.

After Brandon walks off, Mr. C. blows his whistle to get the class going again. Will steps over to me, twirling the volleyball. "That was a killer run. Ready to go again?"

My mouth gapes open. Because of him, I nearly met an early death. Does my life mean nothing to him? "Come on. One more time. I'll bet we can reach fifteen," he says.

I step away. "Leave me the hell alone."

CHAPTER FIVE

I settle down a bit after eating my lunch. Most days, I hate eating by myself, but today it's not so bad. Gives me a chance to think about how lucky I am to have escaped death. I am the zebra who crossed the crocodile-infested river to escape the lion.

Anyway, that's what I'm thinking about when Nick plops down across from me, grinning like a lunatic. I don't think I've ever seen him so happy. This does not bode well for me. "Ooh, you shouldn't have done that. Brandon's going to cream you."

I wave him off. "Come on. It was an accident. I already apologized."

"Hmm...maybe it was, maybe it wasn't."

"You know it was. And Brandon calmed down after, so we're cool."

"Are you cool? Are you really?" His grin rides up around his earlobes like a pair of glasses. I don't know how he has room for the rest of his face. I miss his usual sour expression; this one is freaking me out. "Gee, I don't know, Jake. I wouldn't be so sure about that. When I told Brandon how much you made him look like a fool in front of everybody, he didn't seem too cool about it to me."

I gawk in disbelief. I know Nick doesn't like me, but I didn't think he wanted me dead.

"What the hell?"

"Someone's been needing to knock you down for a long time."

"Dang, Nick. If you hate me so much, why don't you do it?"

His smirk radiates evil. "Brandon will do a better job." Can't argue there. Nick and I are about the same size. Win or lose, I could walk away after a fight with him. But against Brandon? Forget it. The guy's a two-hundred-ton gorilla. He would tear me to shreds.

Hold up. How many pounds are in a ton? OK, I may have overplayed the weight difference, but you get my point. Brandon is freakin' huge. And me? I'm in serious trouble.

The rest of the day is a game of cat and mouse with me in the role of the skittering rodent. I'll say this about Nick: he's evil enough to set me up for certain death, but at least he's arrogant enough to give me a heads up. I scour the hallway between each class, wary of Brandon.

I have a close call on my way to band, but manage to crouch behind a gaggle of eighth-grade girls long enough to sneak past him. Those girls toss me dirty looks, all upturned noses under caked-on eye shadow. Doesn't matter. At least I survive to see another mod.

Dismissal presents a new complication. I stop at my locker. Brandon and I aren't on the same bus, so I figure if I can bolt out of my last class and grab what I need, maybe I can make it to safety. And hopefully I'll be finished before Will gets to his locker. I don't want to deal with him either.

I jump the last bell like a racehorse. I lead the pack and make great time to my locker. Come on, sticky lock. Open. Books in, books out. And done.

"Hey, Jake." I spin around to face Jess. "Did anyone pick you for their group yet?"

Now she's messing with me? Wait, is she serious? "No," I say.

"Good. I need one more for my group. Are you in?"

"Really?" Whoa, way too desperate. "Awesome!" No, way too excited. "I mean, sure that'd be OK." Nailed it.

"Right, so, here's the— "

"Hey, you. What's-your-name." Brandon closes in with Nick in tow. Brandon's jutting forehead reaches me first, followed by his sharp face, broad shoulders, and massive arms. His shirt stretches at the seams when he moves. I don't think I've ever seen him fit properly into anything. It's like he outgrows his clothes as he puts them on. "You think you can make a fool of me, huh?"

My life flashes before my eyes. That went by fast.

"Excuse me," Jess says.

"You think you can get away with it?" Brandon's hands ball into fists the size of armadillos.

"I said, excuse me."

"How 'bout you and me go outside and settle this

right now."

"Hello. I said, excuse me. I'm talking to Jake right now."

Brandon cringes as though she'd doused him with ice water. "Uh, then hurry up?"

"In a minute."

"Did you hear me?" He snarls at her.

"I heard you, Brandon. Now you hear me. *I* am talking to Jake right now, and *you* are interrupting." She pokes him in the chest when she says this like she has a death wish. "Our conversation will take however long it takes. I will not be rushed."

Brandon's eyes go wild. He looks at me like he expects me to help him out. Sure, why not? It's the least I could do.

"You can always kill me tomorrow," I say.

"Fine." Brandon storms away, throwing Nick into a tizzy.

"Wait, where are you going? She's just a girl." Nick glares at us and races after Brandon.

Jess grimaces. "What did you do to set Brandon off?"

"Nothing. Well, nothing much. I hit him in the head with a volleyball. By accident."

"Uh-huh." Jess passes me a folded paper. "Read this over carefully. Our presentation is on the effect of deforestation on Sumatra. I want you to focus on orangutans. Start your research tonight."

No problem. I'll just look it up on Wikipedia.

"And don't just look it up on Wikipedia."

"What? Of course not." Drat.

"Good. The three of us will meet up tomorrow

during class to put our presentation together." She winks. "Assuming you're still alive by then."

I like that she winks at me, even if we are joking about my untimely death. Jess starts to leave, but I call out after her. "Wait a sec. Who's the third person in our group?"

She swings around, a sly smile on her face. "Will."

CHAPTER SIX

After finishing my homework and taking a well-deserved break, I get right into my science project research. And yes, I look up 'orangutan' on Wikipedia, but I also spend a solid hour watching orangutan videos on YouTube. I'm more of a visual learner.

I start with a few BBC Earth documentaries. They're British, so already I'm smarter. That leads me to baby orangutan videos. Those little guys are even cuter than human babies, although that's not saying much. I know most people think human babies are cute, but I find them way too screechy and poopy-smelling. I still remember carrying Emma around. As soon as she smelled bad, I would run straight to Mom. Mom would see me coming and call out, "Go to Daddy. It's Daddy's turn." Emma would yell back, "No. Mommy. Want Mommy!" She always wanted Mom.

Good thing she was done with diapers before Mom died. Our house would have stunk like a latrine.

Thinking about Mom gets me into a self-pity mood, so I click on orangutan orphan videos. Terrible idea. So much for misery loving company. Right when my mood is about to bottom out, I find a video about an orangutan who befriends a hound dog. That directs me to videos of odd animal couples: cat/owl, leopard/bunny, dog/dolphin. By the time Dad comes upstairs, I'm watching cat pouncing fails. "This is your homework?"

"I got distracted."

"OK. I brought home pizza. Mushroom and olive."

Emma and I love mushroom and olive. Once Mom introduced us, we never wanted any other toppings, much to Dad's annoyance. He can't stand mushrooms.

"Why don't you like mushrooms?"

"I have nothing against mushrooms," Dad says, "except for the nasty taste, the slimy texture, and the disgusting smell. I had to drive home with the window open so I didn't hurl. But hey, it's my kid's birthday." He pats me on the back. "Turn off the computer and come downstairs."

"Wait, I want to show you a video."

"Jake."

"Just one."

I type in "Little baby orangutans get scared." In the video, three baby orangutans hover together on a platform, afraid of the macaque monkeys. Near the end, two orangutans hold each other and exclude the third, who has a complete meltdown. The voiceover says, "Lonely Felix has no one to hold onto," in a typical documentary voice, displaying zero emotion.

Orangutans don't have to suffer through middle school, but this is pretty darn close.

Dad watches silently, his forehead wrinkled. When we reach the Felix part, he stops breathing. I'm starting to regret showing him the video. As soon as it's over, I shut down the computer. He puts his arm around my shoulder. "Which orangutan are you?"

"I'm hungry," I say.

CHAPTER SEVEN

We dig into the pizza. Dad uses a fork to pick off the mushrooms and piles them on the side of his plate. We go through our usual tell-me-about-your-day routine. Dad often complains that I can never remember anything about my day, but my memory is not the problem. I just have a hard time trying to come up with something that's not horrible. My day, sanitized for his protection.

After Em describes her recess in minute-by-minute detail, I tell him about volleyball. Obviously, I leave out the part at the end where I'm nearly mauled by a grizzly.

"Will sounds like an interesting person," Dad says. "It's always exciting to meet new people." Dad's just full of wisdom. Last week he told me I should try to be nicer to people. I thanked him for solving middle school.

"I guess."

"OK, guys. My turn. Let me tell you about all the wild craziness today at work." We all laugh. Dad's an optometrist. Nothing remotely wild or crazy ever happens to him at work. While most people would find his job mind-numbingly tedious, Dad enjoys what he does. "I help people see the world clearer," he once told me. "I know it's only one of the many problems in the universe, but it's the one I can solve." Dad can be a bit of a philosopher.

He picks the mushrooms off a new slice of pizza. "No, seriously though," he says. "Let's talk about this weekend. I'll be going out on Saturday."

"On a date?"

"With a friend, yes. Pau Pau will come over and make you zhōu. That's the rice congee dish you guys like. You know the one. Come on, don't look at me like that. You guys like it." We do like it. What we don't like is him leaving us to go out on a date. And what I also don't like is a babysitter.

"We don't need a babysitter," I say.

"She's not a babysitter. She's your Pau Pau, and she wants to come over. She likes to see you guys."

"I don't see why she has to be here."

"Can she bring Mochi?" I glare at Emma. Traitor.

"Sure. I'll ask her."

"And Pocky? And almond cookies?"

"Um, let me talk to her."

"And lychee pudding?"

"Emma, please. Let's not get carried away."

"Seriously," I say. "Why not ask for a red envelope?"

Emma gasps. "Are we getting red envelopes?" Red envelopes contain money, but Emma isn't greedy. She just likes the pretty envelopes.

"Stop it. Both of you. She's not coming over to bribe you."

"Are you sure?" I say.

"Jake. Be nice. She wants to come over and see her grandchildren."

"So you can go on a date to replace her daughter?"

Dad pounds his fist on the table. Emma and I freeze. He closes his eyes for several seconds before lifting his hand. "Listen, Jake, we've talked about this. Mom died four years ago. No one is replacing her. I get one night a week for adult time. I do not need your permission. Pau Pau can come over to see her grandchildren whenever she wants. She doesn't need your permission either. None of this is up to you."

Like I don't know. Nothing is ever up to me. And I'm not OK with that.

"Daddy?" Emma has curled into a ball.

"Yes, honey."

"That was scary."

"I'm sorry about hitting the table. I think the mushroom smell has gone to my brain. I'm getting delirious."

Emma giggles. "What's delirious?"

"It's like confused. I don't know which end is up. I'm so delirious, I think a monkey has attached herself to your neck."

Emma giggles some more. She never tires of this game.

"Daddy, that's Beenie."

"What? Beenie, what are you doing at the dinner table? Uh-oh. I hope I brought home enough pizza. She doesn't like mushrooms, does she?"

"Beenie *loves* mushrooms."

"Good, she can have mine."

"I want some, too," I say.

"Sure. Nasty fungus for everybody."

Dad distributes his mushroom pile.

After dinner, there's no cake or singing. We go straight to the presents. I may hate birthdays, but I'm cool with the getting-stuff part. I'm not an idiot.

Emma's gift is a card she made. On the front she wrote, "Happy You Know What." I open the card and stare at a picture of Beenie. I can't believe it. Why in the heck would she think I'd want a drawing of her stuffed monkey?

"Isn't it nice?" Dad says. "She spent a long time drawing that."

Dad and I stare at each other and have a silent conversation.

Thank your sister.

Why?

She put a lot of thought and effort into the card.

She drew her stuffed monkey. What does this have to do with me?

She loves Beenie, and she loves you. In her mind, this makes sense.

Doesn't mean I have to thank her.

Yes, it does. Do it now.

Forget it.

Did you want my gift? I can still return it.

Fine.

"Thanks, Em."

She leans in to hug me. I shift my body so she only gets my arm.

"Happy you know what," she says and runs out of the kitchen with Beenie.

"Was that so hard?" Dad asks.

"Kinda."

"When you go upstairs, I want you to put the card away in your room. I don't want her to find the card in the trash."

"Whatever."

"No, not whatever. You don't want to hurt your sister's feelings."

I really hate birthdays.

"Are you ready for your gift?"

"From you and Mom."

"Yes." He puts the gift on the table. "She and I talked about what age this would be appropriate, and we decided on twelve."

More like she decided on twelve and he just agreed with her but whatever. Since I'm twelve now, this works for me. I tear into the wrapping paper, which isn't wrapping paper at all, but some kind of optometry form he uses at work. "I think you forgot to write 'birthday wrapping paper' on your list," I say.

"I'll be sure to put it on there before Emma's birthday since she actually cares how I wrap her presents." He's right. I don't care. In fact, I prefer his boring work paper to the flashy birthday wrapping with flying cakes and overwrought exclamation marks.

"It's a cell phone," he says, unnecessarily since I'm staring at it. "I got you a card with sixty minutes. You can take the phone to school and call me if you need to get picked up or if there are any problems. This thing is cool. You can even take pictures and shoot videos with it."

"Yes, Dad. I know how phones work."

Dad groans. "Only your generation would think that's what phones are supposed to do."

That's Dad. He used to think he was technologically advanced. One time at dinner, Dad told us this long story about how he was the first person in his family to figure out how to program the VCR. He had to teach everybody else. The whole time, Em and I kept looking at each other. When he finished, we finally asked him what a VCR was. He deflated like a balloon, even making the same sad sound with his lips, Pbpbpbpbpbpbp.

"So, do you like the phone?"

"It's great. Thanks, Mom. You, too, Dad."

He laughs and kisses my head. He's getting good at doing that before I can pull away. He's a stealth head kisser. If the government ever weaponized him, we could kiss the heads of everyone in the Middle East before they knew what hit them. And they'd have new glasses.

I feel halfway decent when I go to bed. As birthdays go, this one wasn't too awful. Sure, I'm likely to be a corpse by the end of school tomorrow, but today I've got a phone. Not bad.

Before I drift off, I think about Connor. That loony kangaroo may be bent on my destruction, but he's a refreshing change from my usual nightmare about the turtles. Massive and creepy, the turtles guard the basement to prevent me from seeing Mom. In the dream, she's trapped down there. I'm not afraid of turtles in real life but during the dream, I experience absolute terror. Those monstrous snappers have forced me awake in a cold sweat more times than I can remember. Even now the turtles unsettle me, so I think about Mom instead, a time many birthdays ago.

We go to the zoo in the city. They have this miniature train you can ride on. I've never been on it before, and I can't stop talking about it while we walk around. I'm excited because I think there'll be interesting views of the animals, but the train just loops through the woods. You really can't see much besides trees and fences. I get bored halfway through, so Mom and I look at the clouds and pretend we can see new animals up there. A fluffy platypus and a white screech owl. A snake who's eaten a rhinoceros. We laugh the whole way back. I laughed a lot back then.

I want to ride around again the moment we get back, but she convinces me that we can see the clouds just fine from outside the train. I say, *OK, but on my next birthday I want to go up into the sky with you. Sure,* she says, *we'll jump the clouds together.* We would have, too, if she hadn't died. And don't tell me it's impossible. She would have figured out a way. You don't know her like I do. Did.

CHAPTER EIGHT

I find myself in a grassy field extending before me in all directions. The blades bend with the breeze, sending ripples cascading across the pasture. But I will not be lulled by the calm surroundings. I pull the dream into focus, sharpening the colors.

"Anybody here?"

A creature pops out of a hole and stands at attention. Its fur is brown except for the black at the tip of its tail. I know this creature well. Prairie dogs are adorable. The sentry barks and other brown critters pop up from holes in the grass until a vast array of pups stand before me. They greet me with hundreds of squeaky barks.

"Hi, everybody. I guess there are no orangutans on

the prairie. I must have taken a wrong turn at Albuquerque."

"Are you looking for me?" I spin towards the voice behind me. Stepping out of the forest, one I'm certain was not there a moment ago, is an orangutan. He has no cheek pads, so he must be a young guy like me. "The name's Owen," he says. "Have you got any root beer?"

"Um, no. How would I have root beer?"

"Try thinking it loudly."

Sure, why not? Root beer.

Nothing happens.

"Louder, you have to think louder than that."

ROOT BEER.

A bottle of root beer appears in my hands. That is too awesome. I pass it to Owen who rips off the cap and flops on his back, sucking the soda with his lips. He chugs half the bottle before rolling back up to offer me some. I pass. Ape-flavored spittle is not my thing.

"You're him," Owen says. "I knew it." He circles around me on his knuckles, whooping and hollering. The prairie dogs scamper underground. He stretches his neck to bring his lips closer to my ear. I expect a whisper but instead I get this:

"You're the dreamer!" His breath is fruity with a hint of bark. I shush him.

"What's the matter?"

"There's a certain kangaroo I want to avoid."

"Connor? You've met Connor? Oh, don't even get me started."

"It's OK, you don't have to – "

"Connor's a menace. One time, I got into the storage bin, and I chugged four bottles of root beer, one after the other. That got me tipsy, of course, so I stumbled around slurring my words until a certain kangaroo-who-shall-remain-nameless tells me root beer is not really a type of beer and I should quit my foolishness. But why would they call it root beer if it's not a type of beer? That's like saying a gummy bear isn't a type of bear. Ridiculous, don't you agree?"

"Yes. That is all completely ridiculous."

"Right? So, while he's chewing me out for the foolishness, I leap into the trees and swing far away from him. I go fast and high, but when I reach my nest from the night before, he's up there waiting for me. And he says it again, 'Quit your foolishness this instant.' Freaky, huh? But I tell him. I will never stop my foolishness, this instant or any other."

Flopping on his back again, Owen sucks the bottle dry. He lifts a finger, and we both wait. It doesn't take long. A massive belch vibrates his lips. This guy would make a great trumpet player.

"Good one," I say.

Owen leaps up. "One time I met a dead Greek guy who said an unexamined life isn't worth living, but I'd much rather examine insects, you know? I'd rather discover meaning in life than discover the meaning of life. Especially if it means I'd have to wear a toga."

He blows a raspberry. A wet one. I step aside to avoid the spray.

"Hold up, I changed my mind. I'll wear the toga. Hey, you know where I can get a toga this time of night?"

TOGA.

A toga appears in my hands. I pass it to Owen.

"Sweet." He wraps himself up. "This really brings

out my fur." When he bounces his head, his hair whips around his face. He kinda reminds me of Will when he does that. Now that I think about it, Owen's voice has a similar breezy California twang.

"Say, what do you think of my 'do?" Owen tugs at the fur on his head. "Should I grow it out more?" The guy's an orange shag carpet, but the question seems important to him.

"Sure. Why not?"

His smile brightens. "Great. I will. Hey, we should be friends. Let's hang out."

"Aren't we hanging out now?"

"No, I mean in the trees." He drops a hairy hand on my shoulder. "I'm just joking. I know you're not an orangutan. I won't hold that against you. My mom taught me that creatures come in all shapes and sizes. You should be nice to everyone, even the frail pinkish ones."

"I'm pink only on my father's side," I say. "Frail on both."

"Come on, let's do something fun. Whatever you want – sky's the limit."

The sky. That's a great idea. "Can we go cloud jumping?"

Owen shushes me. "Not so loud. Connor hates that. We'll have to sneak in, but yeah, we can do it."

Owen and I continue down the path. The way he walks all hunched over, we're about the same height.

"Only the red portal will lead us to the clouds," he says. "To get there, we'll have to find a way through the three-hundred-feet tunnel. That's the tricky part."

"Three hundred feet? That's not too long." My math

is fuzzy even when I'm awake, but I'm pretty sure the length is less than a football field.

"Not three hundred foot, three hundred feet. Smelly ones with bunions and craggy toenails. It's just up the road."

I can already hear the stamping. When we round the bend, I see the tunnel. Black birds perch at the opening, their beady eyes staring inside. Within the tunnel, disembodied feet fight over a canvas ball. "What the heck are they doing?"

"Playing football."

Right. Dumb question. "Will they let us through?"

"Let's see." Owen steps into the opening and is pelted by a foot swarm. He tries again, barreling forward with a lowered shoulder but doesn't make it any further inside. "Guess not. Do you have any ideas?"

"Let's try to take them out one at a time." I leap at the closest foot and lug it out of the tunnel. It's clammy and smells like, well, feet.

Owen joins in. After a few minutes, we've made two dirt trails leading to two piles of feet, but we've hardly made a dent in the foot swarm that guards the tunnel. "This is going to take forever," I say.

"You're right. We're just dragging our feet."

I groan. "I totally set you up for that one."

"Any more ideas, or should we give up?"

No way am I giving up. There must be a solution. If brute force won't work, we need to try something else. What would make feet *want* to get away from us? Oh, of course.

"Owen, what kind of birds are those?"

"I'm not sure. Black birds who like football?"

Ravens. These birds are the key.

"We need feathers," I say. "Think you can scare some

loose?"

"No problem." Owen leaps at the tunnel's edge, throwing the birds into a panic. Black feathers flutter down.

"Grab as many feathers as you can and let's go."

We tickle our way through the tunnel. After the first several feet, it's easy going. I mean feet as in distance, not feet as in feet. There are a good twenty feet per foot. OK, maybe it's time we switched to the metric system. How many feet in a meter? Nah, skip it.

While I'm psyched to go cloud jumping, I'm already having a blast in the tunnel. Most of the feet skitter away, but a few of the smaller feet keep coming back just to get tickled again. It's weirdly cute. I can tell Owen's also enjoying himself; he keeps flashing his toothy grin.

We finally reach the end of the tunnel and break through the last few feet. I mean feet as in – actually, that works either way. Owen points up the path.

"We did it! We've reached the red portal. You're going to love cloud jumping. Very few people die once they get good at it."

"Wait, what?"

He never gets the chance to answer. Connor hops in front of the portal, followed by a squadron of creatures who block our path. They're a zoo animal menagerie: giraffes, elephants, penguins, zebras, leopards, and so on. No pandas, though. This must not be the gang from the National Zoo.

Connor hops towards Owen. "Hold up, why are you wearing a toga? Were you drinking root beer?" Connor sniffs him.

I laugh. "Oh, you're so busted! Hey, wait a minute. That makes no sense. Why would wearing a toga mean you drank root beer? Connor wasn't even there when we had that conversation."

The animals murmur among themselves. The flamingos beat their wings.

Owen thumps me in the chest. "It's a dream, remember? You're overthinking this."

"Right. Hey, sorry, everybody." The hippos slump down on the dirt. The warthogs snort.

"Really, my bad. Let's start over."

"No worries," Connor says. "This is Owen's fault for bringing you here. And he knows the punishment." Connor scratches his belly with one hand and motions with the other. The big cats step forward. They bare their teeth and claws.

Owen makes a break for the woods and leaps from tree to tree. The cheetahs cut off his escape. He's quick but running out of options – and branches. I grab a huge leaf and call him over to me. He comes without hesitation. I sure hope this works. When he reaches me, I cover us with the leaf just as two tigers are about to close in. We hear growling and gnashing over us but are unharmed. "How did you know this would work?"

"Dream rules," I say. "You're always safe under a blanket." Crickets swarm under the leaf. Their shrill chirps are deafening. Owen pops a few of the buggers into his mouth. I want to cover my ears, but I don't want to risk dropping the leaf.

"See you tomorrow night," he says between chews.

"Are you going somewhere?"

"No. You are."

A giant hand appears by my head and yanks the leaf from my grip.

I scream.

Dad cringes. He turns off the alarm, silencing the crickets. We stare at each other. Please don't ask me to explain this. "Are you OK?"

"Sure," I say, "I'm fine."

Fine, except for the bloodthirsty cats with laser-sharp claws that nearly slashed me into bits. What could be worse? Then I remember I have school today and must face Brandon.

Drat. I hate it when I answer my own question.

CHAPTER NINE

The entire time I'm brushing my teeth, I can't stop thinking about last night. That dream was such a rush. Sure, it was a bit freaky toward the end, but I'm new to this whole concept of being awake during the dream. I'll work it out. Thanks to this weird new power, I no longer have to worry about getting dragged into the basement with the turtles. No more nightmares for me, at least not when I'm sleeping. I still have to deal with middle school. And Brandon. Maybe that won't be so bad today. Maybe he and I can talk man-to-man. Or, you know, mouse-to-elephant. Squeak, squeak.

When I go downstairs for breakfast, I get my little sister her Elmo bowl before she even asks. What can I say? I'm in a better mood.

I pour my cereal. Emma inches her bowl toward me.

She and Beenie stare at me with matching brown eyes. She's pushing it, but whatever. I pour her the cereal. She smiles and glances at the milk. Holy moo cow. Every morning. You'd think she'd want to learn how to do things by herself.

Steady. One problem at a time. I pour her the milk.

A few minutes later, Dad swings into the kitchen while pressing a hand against his wrinkled shirt. He heads for the refrigerator and tears the list off the pad. "Last call. I'm food shopping after work." He waves the list in the air. I shrug. Emma grins. Beenie hangs around Emma's neck. "Everything OK down here? You three are awfully quiet this morning."

"That's true," I say. "Usually Beenie won't shut up." Emma giggles. I enjoy making her laugh. We haven't gotten along in a while. I suppose I should try being nicer to her more often. It's not all that difficult when I'm not so angry.

Dad beams. "It's great to see – no, I don't want to jinx it. Emma, we need to leave as soon as you're finished. I have a meeting this morning. Jake, do you have your new phone?"

"In my bag." Emma finishes her last spoonful of cereal and carries her bowl to the sink.

"And your glasses?"

"I'll put them on before I go."

Emma unhooks Beenie from her neck and carefully places her on the stairs. This way, she can run right to Beenie after school and scoop her back up. Seriously, I've seen her do this.

Dad lifts Emma's book bag and takes her hand. When they reach the door, he turns around. "You wear your glasses during class, right?"

"Only if I want to see the board."

"Good, good." They head out, but a moment later, Dad pops his head back in.

"Just to be clear. Was that a yes?"

CHAPTER TEN

My mood falters the moment the bus pulls up to the school, so I try to think positive thoughts. I'm in a science group. At least Nick can't harass me about that.

When I reach my locker, I remember how I left things with Will. I guess I should make up with him. And maybe I'd better stay out of Brandon's way, just in case.

"Hey, you. Jake." I spin around. So much for staying out of Brandon's way. I hardly have time to blink before Brandon backs me up against my locker.

"You and me. After school." He smacks his fist into his hand. "You're dead." Brandon hovers so close I can barely see Nick smirking off to the side. "And you better not wuss out this time, you hear me? Or you're dead." Brandon jams a thick finger in my face. How is this hulking lump even a seventh grader? "You hear me?"

"I hear you." When he removes his finger from my

face, I step away, but not before he shoves me hard. My shoulder clips the metal lockers, generating a clang that reverberates down the hallway. That gets everyone's attention. We all watch Brandon puff his chest like a preening peacock. Nick doesn't even try to mask an evil grin.

Brandon struts off with Nick close behind. I go back to getting my books together, acting real casual. No biggie, just a friendly chat, nothing to see here. All the while, I focus my energy on keeping it together. "Are you all right?" I didn't even hear Will come over.

"I'm fine," I say. That's not a complete lie. Thanks to the adrenaline rush, my shoulder tingles but isn't all that sore. I continue to gather my books at a deliberate pace. Acting nonchalant is tough with shaky hands. My anger builds, but I hold it in.

By the time I make it to homeroom, a massive cramp has set in. Just lifting my arm causes my muscles to spasm. Lightning ripples across my upper back. I ease into my chair. Right when I think it can't get any worse, I hear Nick's taunting voice. "I want to know, Norman. Did anyone join your loser group or not? Come on, what's your problem? Just tell me." I guess his target is Norman now. Nick must figure he's got me covered already.

"Don't tell me you couldn't get anyone. Really? There's not one person in this class as lame as you?" Nick looks right at me. "Not even one?" I fume. This is the same stupid taunt from yesterday. He's phoning it in. Being bested by such a lame jerk infuriates me. If this were one of my dreams, I'd probably think up a way to outsmart him. I wish I could go back to the dream world where I could jump atop the clouds far away from middle school, where nothing and nobody can ever truly hurt me. But no. I'm stuck here in my miserable reality.

I tune Nick out. The only other conversation going on is the one the girls in the back are having, so I focus on that. They're arguing about what group to join and who gets to pair off with which friend. The conversation is no more than a series of accusations and recriminations. I let their inane babbling wash over me anyway. Beats listening to Nick.

Between my shoulder's throbbing and the girls' bickering, I have an epiphany of sorts. I think I can solve the girls' problem and at least one of mine. I'm usually too nervous to talk to them. Mixing it up with the popular girls involves tolerating a degree of haughtiness I'd much rather avoid. But knowing I might not survive the day provides me with a curious bravery. I truly have nothing to lose.

I make my way to the back and stand before them. They don't acknowledge my existence. Too bad I never learned their names. That would probably help right about now. "I have an idea," I say in their general direction. They still ignore me. I try again louder. "I said, I think I have a solution to your problem."

The girls quiet down and stare at me. If I had to describe their expression in one word, I would go with *unimpressed*. Fair enough. "You should ask Norman if you can be in his group."

Now I would go with *scorn*. Or maybe *contempt*. No wait, definitely *disgust*.

"Is that supposed to be funny?" The lead popular girl contorts her face in a most unattractive way. "You think I should be in the loser group?"

"It wouldn't really be the loser group if you were in it."

I can tell she likes my answer, so I keep talking. "Here's what I was thinking. I'll bet Norman finished the entire project last night by himself. Really. I wouldn't put it past him. So if you're looking for a group where you don't have to do much work and are guaranteed a good grade, I don't think you can do any better than Norman's group."

If this were a cartoon, four tiny dim bulbs would appear over the pretty heads surrounding me. Once the lead popular girl moves, they all rush over to besiege Norman, pleading for him to choose them to join his group. Nick's taunts trail off.

I stroll back to my seat. The girls paw at a delighted yet terrified Norman. Nick's jaw plunges to the floor. Why didn't I have my phone ready? This could have been my first YouTube post. "Taunting fail." Yeah, I'd totally watch that.

Will raises an eyebrow. I act casual. "Pretty wild, huh?" He doesn't say anything. Instead, he puts his hands together and bows. I'm not really sure what that means, but I think we're back on good terms again. I point to Nick. "Check him out. If it's stunned silent like a duck."

Will laughs.

Nick doesn't react. I don't know if he even heard me. In fact, I'm not sure he's still breathing. If he could turn green with envy, Nick would be a bullfrog. Hold up, make that a toad. I know that kills the whole green thing, but I still see Nick as more of a toad.

"Please, girls, one at a time," Norman says. "I am limited to two choices. You may each make your case as to why I should choose you, and then I'll make my decision."

Yes, Norman has reverted to his usual insufferable self, but what of it? Everyone deserves a moment of glory. Maybe one day I'll have my moment. Better happen soon, though. I don't expect to make it past the end of school today.

CHAPTER ELEVEN

After the bell, Mrs. Vespa has us break into groups to work on our projects. Jess, Will, and I compare notes. Turns out they wrote their notes down, unlike me. Jess frowns, but when I demonstrate my vast orangutan knowledge, she settles down. Which is a relief to me, although I find it disturbing how much I care what she thinks.

Oh, and she smells like strawberries today. I wonder whether she ate strawberries for breakfast or she switched her shampoo. While I'm trying to figure out a way to casually sniff her hair, I realize she's waiting for me to say something. "Sorry, what?"

"I said, how does deforestation affect the orangutans?"

"They, well, they live in the forest, so their home is shrinking."

"Right, but who is doing the deforestation, why are

they doing it, and how can we stop them?"

"Um." Yeah, that goes a bit beyond my research from last night. "I thought you wanted me to look up orangutans."

Jess rolls her eyes. "Did you even read the paper I gave you?"

Her disappointment floors me. This is not my fault. She told me to look up orangutans. How was I supposed to know she wanted me to read the paper?

"When I handed you the paper, I told you to read it over carefully."

Oh. Yeah.

"Really, Jake? All you had to do was follow my directions."

"Fine. I'll research it tonight."

"Our presentation is Monday. We're supposed to put this together today."

"I don't think any of us are ready," Will says. "We should get together this weekend to finish up."

Jess settles against the desk and purses her lips. My body tingles in an unexpected way. I don't think I've ever noticed her lips before. Great, now I'm thinking about her lips. Like I need another distraction. "Will's right," she says. "We need to brainstorm this weekend, so we can be prepared. Jake, are you listening?"

"Yes," I say, although mostly I was staring at her lips. I had never noticed how expressive they are. I especially enjoyed the way she said "prepared."

"Then what did I say?"

"Um...prepared?"

She tilts her head. "At least you got one word. Are you all right?"

"He had a run-in with Brandon this morning," Will says.

I clear my throat, but he doesn't get my cue.

"Brandon slammed him against the lockers."

Jess gasps. Although her empathetic look is an improvement over her annoyed look, I really don't want to talk about this.

"Can we get back to the orangutans?" I say. "I think I did see, I mean *read* something about multinational corporations cutting and burning down the forests."

"Why would they do that?"

"To make money, I guess. I don't remember exactly how that makes them money. I focused on orangutans; I wasn't paying that close attention, I mean *reading* that carefully."

Jess rests her hands on her hips. "You just watched a bunch of videos, didn't you?"

And we're back to her annoyed look. Which annoys me.

"What did you come up with? Why am I responsible for figuring everything out?"

"What are you talking about? I wrote all this down." She holds up her notes.

"That's a lot of words. Is there something in there that answers the question? Or solves the problem? I mean, is that even our assignment? Are we really supposed to solve this in four days? Seriously, you read the paper, what exactly are we supposed to do here?"

"I don't think she expects us to solve the problem, just offer solutions. I think. Let me check."

Jess unfolds the paper. Her lips move when she

reads. I really need to stop staring.

"I'm not totally sure. Let me check with Mrs. Vespa. I'll be right back."

After Jess leaves, Will nods at me. "You did good today," he says.

"Jess doesn't think so."

"Huh? No, not that. I mean what you did for Norman. Getting those girls to beg him to be in his group." He chuckles to himself. "That was wild. I don't know how you pulled it off, but you definitely made his day." He lifts his hand before I can respond. "Don't deny it. I saw you talk to those girls before they came over. I know it was all you. That was a very cool thing you did." He puts his fist out and I bump it with mine. I should be flattered, but I'm uncomfortable with how much credit he's giving me. He talks again before I can argue. "Sorry about gym yesterday."

"Nah," I say. "That was my fault. I was off balance for that last spike. There's no way you could have gotten it."

"Right, I know. I mean after, when you got mad at me. I didn't understand until I saw what happened at the lockers. I had no idea how crazy Brandon was. What he did this morning was horrible. You should tell the principal."

"The principal? Are you insane? That would turn one beating into several."

He bobs his head from side to side, blond hair flapping. "Yeah, maybe. Your call. I leave it to you. I know you'll figure a way out of this."

"You think I can figure a way out of this?"

"Sure. I've been watching you. You're the sharpest kid in the class."

"You must be joking." I hike my thumb towards

Norman.

"Norman's book-smart but otherwise pretty clueless. Not like you. I got the picture early on. You're the guy I want on my side. What you did this morning clinches it."

Will claps my back. I flinch. I wish he'd done that on the other side.

"Oh, sorry. I forgot. But really, you did what needed to be done. And you didn't even try to take any credit. No, don't worry, I won't say anything. You can be secretly magnanimous if that's what you're going for." He smiles. "Man, that was killer. Whatever you told those girls worked perfectly."

Yeah, it did, except all I wanted to do was get Nick back. I hadn't considered Norman's feelings at all. Which makes me no better than Nick. Less of a jerk maybe but no less petty. Now Will thinks I'm, like, noble or something.

It's kinda weird to have someone give me too much credit. To assume my best intentions. It's a good weird, though. I just hope I can live up to Will's inflated view of me, to be worthy of his praise.

I wonder if Will could be right. About the other thing, I mean – could I figure a way to convince Brandon not to kill me? I suppose it's worth a try. Maybe I'll look for him before lunch. Why not? Then if I don't get killed, I'll move on to saving the orangutans, solving the energy crisis, and achieving world peace.

Simple.

CHAPTER TWELVE

Today's a B day so at least I don't have gym, but that just makes it harder to figure out how to find Brandon. Searching for Brandon in the hallway strikes me as insane, especially after I spent so much effort avoiding him yesterday. I'd have more success diving into the Atlantic to hunt a great white shark while armed with only a pea shooter. But at this point, what do I have to lose?

I spot him alone at his locker. It's now or never. "Hey, Brandon." I say it so cheerfully Brandon looks around like I must have meant some other Brandon.

"What do you want?"

"I wasn't sure what the plan was for after school. Did you want me to show up?"

"Huh? Yeah, that's what I said."

"Oh, OK. I wasn't sure. It almost seemed like you

didn't want me to. You know, from the mixed messages."

He scans the hallway, maybe thinking there's a teacher nearby and I'm setting him up. If so, he's only half right. "I said if you didn't show up, I'd kill you."

"Right, I got that part, but then you also said if I *did* show up, you'd kill me."

"Yeah?"

"Don't you see the problem? If I'm dead either way, why would I show up? I mean, what's my motivation?" I can almost see the gears in his brain grind against each other. Brandon shakes off the confusion. And by that, I mean he literally shakes his head.

"I don't know. Nick said this would work." Nick. I knew it. Time for a new plan.

"Do you always do what Nick tells you?"

Brandon lunges for my shirt and yanks me closer. "What the hell is that supposed to mean?"

"I didn't mean anything by it; that's just what Nick says. I didn't think it was true at all."

He releases my shirt. He's clearly furious but hopefully not so much with me anymore.

My heart pounds against my chest. When I speak again, my voice warbles, but at least I get all the words out.

"It's weird, you know. I told Nick yes, I hit you with a volleyball – by accident, of course – but I thought you and I could work something out to even the score that didn't involve you killing me. Nick says no, Brandon will do what I tell him, and I want you dead. And I'm like, what? Brandon's not going to do whatever you tell him. But then you come over this morning and prove him right. I really had no idea that he has so much power over you."

Brandon hyperventilates. I see I've touched a nerve. "Nick was all proud of himself. He considers you his personal lap dog. Hey, I know, I couldn't believe it either. That's why I thought I'd check with you. Just to make sure this is what you really what. So, what's the plan? Are we going to do what Nick says, or do you want to come up with something else?"

Brandon's chest heaves forward and he lets out a roar. He slams his fist into the locker, creating a sonic boom that rattles every eardrum in a two-block radius. "What do you think I should do?"

Wow, I was not expecting him to ask me. "I don't want to be like Nick and tell you what to do. I think you should think of something yourself."

Brandon slams his locker shut. "I need to think about this."

"That's cool. You know, today wasn't great for me anyway. Let me know when you figure something out. No rush."

Brandon storms down the hallway. Students clear a path.

I walk away, impressed I'm able to walk at all. My body twitches as though I had chugged a case of energy drinks. That's the second time today. I hope it isn't possible to overdose on adrenaline. I slip into the boys' bathroom to settle down.

The rest of the day is quiet, eerily quiet. I take no chances, keeping a careful watch for Brandon until the final bell. After I stop by my locker, I zip through the halls like a dragonfly, forward, backward, diagonally, until I reach the outside air and leap into the safety of my bus. I plop down on the seat and rest my head against the window.

Against the odds, I survived another day of middle school. And today's Friday. Life doesn't get much better than this.

I hear a commotion outside the bus, but I don't link it to my situation until I recognize Nick's voice. He's screaming my name. Like an idiot, I stand up and look out the window.

Nick points. When Brandon sees me, he rushes over and bangs on the bus. If his plan is to smash a hole in the metal and climb in, he just might succeed. "I'm going to get you, Jake. No more tricks. You hear me? I'll get you next time. You're so dead. You hear me? You hear me?"

I hear him. Everyone on the bus hears him, and they all gawk at me. Kneeling on the seat in front of me, a sixth grader stares with eyes so wide, I wonder if his eyeballs will pop out. For a second, I think he's going to say something encouraging, to empathize with the plight of a fellow small person. But no, this is middle school. "Oh, man. That guy's going to kill you!"

Yeah, thanks, kid. Tell me something I don't know.

CHAPTER THIRTEEN

I don't say much during dinner and not just because Emma goes on and on about her art class. These last two days have really worn me out. Listening to Emma's step-by-step description of macaroni sculptures doesn't help much either. I just want this day to end so I can go back to the dream world. I've had about enough of today.

After dinner, we watch an episode of my show from Animal Planet, and one of Emma's shows from some kiddie network. I don't know the show's name, but I think it's for preschoolers. It involves cutesy voices and frequent giggling. If you watch it for more than a few seconds, your brain will ooze out of your ears. Emma is somehow immune to the danger. She squeals with joy and bounces Beenie on her knee. Dad has his arm around her. I play on my phone, careful not to look up.

There's this game I found called Orb Quash. It's basically like every other game ripped off Mario Brothers, where you have to jump over obstacles and stuff, but the cool thing is you can jump into a ball and use it as a shield. If the ball pops, you can keep going without it. That's key since you get only one life before the game resets to the beginning. It's ridiculously addictive.

"All right. Time to wash up."

"Hang on, I've never gotten this far...and now I'm dead."

After Dad puts Emma to bed, he comes in to check on me. Obviously I don't really go to bed at the same time as my little sister, but she gets cranky if she thinks I'm staying up later.

Dad tries out Orb Quash. He dies ten times in less than a minute. That's got to be a record. "Why does this cave opening have spikes on it? This game makes no sense."

"You can get past it if you're in a ball."

"Mine keeps popping before I get there."

"You're bouncing at the wrong angle. See, you tapped too early."

He hands me my phone. "I don't know how you can stand this game. It's so frustrating."

"I like it. Watch, it's all in the timing. See, I'm in the ball...got it, in the cave."

He kisses my head. I avoided the spikes but couldn't dodge that.

"I'll check on you later."

I play only a few more times before plugging in my phone and curling up under the blanket. My mind races through my day. Ugh, I don't want to think about Brandon and Nick. I focus on Mom. My thoughts drift to our last zoo trip.

Four summers ago, barely a month before Mom died, we go to the National Zoo. We walk all the way up the hill from the lower parking lot to the panda house. Dad carries Emma most of the way. Mom leans on him toward the end.

Despite Mom trying to hide it, I notice her gasp for air. She seems less winded after we crest the hill and make our way down the trail where you can watch the pandas.

Emma bounces on Dad's chest, straining to see, but pandas don't really do much and it doesn't take long before Emma gets bored. She insists on going to Kid's Farm, all the way back down the hill. I notice Mom wince. I speak up right away. *I want to stay here with Mom.*

After Dad and Emma leave, Mom and I spend nearly an hour watching the panda do a whole lot of nothing. We decide to rename her. I suggest *Nap Nap* and Mom proposes *Sit Sit.* Finally, that adorable black-and-white fluffball settles in with a bamboo pile. We agree on *Chomp Chomp.* Or however you say it in Chinese.

When we stop laughing, Mom asks me if I want to move on. *It's getting late,* she says. *Didn't you want to see the great apes and the reptiles?*

Yes, and the invertebrates and the small mammals and everything else, but so what? They're not going anywhere.

No rush, I say. *Whenever you feel up to it.*

She doesn't respond, so I watch the panda until I realize Mom is staring at me. *What?* I say. She runs her hand from the back of my head to my neck. *Were you staying here for me?* Her eyelids flicker. I worry she's angry with me, so I talk fast. *I thought you could use a rest. You looked tired. I'm sorry. We can leave if you want.*

Mom veers away. She crouches over and shakes. I worry she's upset with me, but she still has her arm around me, hugging me tight. I find this confusing until she turns back. Her eyes are red. Tears stream down her face. She opens her mouth, but is unable to speak. I ask her a question. *How sick are you?*

She doesn't answer for a long time. Finally, she wipes her eyes and tells me it will all be OK, but I know it won't. Suddenly terrified, I can no longer hold back my tears. Mom cries with me. The panda chomps on bamboo. The crowd streams past us, more interested in the panda squatting in the enclosure than two people huddled together, hanging on to the railing, sharing a fleeting moment in time.

Before long, we wipe our tears and leave. We don't get far down the path before we see Dad pushing Emma up the hill on a wheelchair. A woman in a zoo uniform follows.

Dad explains how Emma got tired and this nice lady let them borrow a wheelchair so he can push Emma around. Oh, and she wants to sit on Mom's lap. Emma jumps out and Mom settles into the chair. Emma climbs back up. The woman whispers something to Mom and Mom thanks her. Dad pushes Mom and Emma, still acting all jolly. He keeps going on and on about how the nice lady let them borrow this wheelchair for Emma to ride in.

Finally, Mom squeezes Dad's arm. *Stop. Jake knows. He knew the whole time.*

Except I didn't exactly. I just thought she was sick. I never truly believed she was going to die, not then and not until the day she did. What I do know for sure is that was the last time I cried about anything. Even through the funeral, despite everyone else blubbering away, I didn't cry. Why bother? I already cried with Mom. No point in doing it again.

CHAPTER FOURTEEN

I find myself walking along a path in a forest. I quickly wrest control of my dream-self and view my surroundings. A river rushes nearby. A faint wind brushes against my hair.

"Anybody there?"

Anybody there?

The echo rumbles from deep within the forest. I see no one. The voice sounds familiar, kinda like my voice but deeper.

"Echo."

Echo.

Why do people always say "echo" when they hear an echo? Lame.

"How do I get out of here?"

How do I get out of here?

I concentrate harder, but I can't seem to leave this

place. The breeze picks up. I shiver. I wish I could do more than move my body. Oh yeah, I can conjure things up. I focus on one word.

OWEN.

Down the path, I see Owen barreling toward me on his knuckles.

I wave. "I sure am glad to see you."

I sure am glad to see you.

"I'm glad I found you," Owen says, rising to his full height. "Most people freak out in Echo Forest."

I listen, but I don't hear an echo.

"I'm from here. There's no echo when I talk."

I shrug it off. "I wasn't freaked out."

I was getting nervous until you showed up.

"Hey, what? That's not what I said."

Hey, what? That's not what I said.

"The voice doesn't echo what you say," Owen explains. "It echoes what you think."

"But...that's not what I was thinking."

But...I didn't want you to know that's what I was thinking.

"Hey!"

Hey!

"It's all right. Nobody likes it here." He flops down on his haunches. "I don't get many visitors."

I can see why. That echo makes me feel exposed, even more than when I was about to go on stage in my underwear. Still, we can't help where we're from.

"Don't sweat it. It's not so bad here."

This place makes me uncomfortable, but I enjoy hanging out with you.

"Oh, thanks, Jake. You're a good guy." My body flushes. Why does the truth embarrass me? I don't know what to say, which is probably just as well. The less I say in this place the better.

"Come on." Owen motions down the path. "I'll show you the way out."

We walk in silence. Time is vague in dreams, so I have no idea how long we do this. I notice the trees repeat every twenty feet or so: same position, same order, same color. It's like walking in one of those old cartoons on Boomerang.

Owen jabs me with his elbow. "How's your project going with Jess?"

"It's tough. She's kind of a pain."

It's tough. I kind of like her.

"What! Oh, come on!"

What! Oh, come on!

Owen laughs. If you've ever heard an ape laugh, you know how disturbing this is. "Is she cute?"

"Ew, gross."

Her lips are nice. I like her funky hair.

I glare into the forest. "You better shut up."

You better stop embarrassing me.

"I do not think that."

I will not admit I think that.

I groan. Maybe Jess has funky hair, but I don't like her. Not like - that's crazy. The stupid echo is completely wrong.

"You're completely wrong."

I find myself thinking about Jess a lot.

OK, enough of this. I'm burning the forest down.

BLOWTORCH. A blowtorch appears in my hands. I fire that baby up.

"We're here. Come on." Owen swings a hairy arm around my waist and pulls me through a portal. The forest vanishes, replaced by a deep blue. We stand on a spongy substance covered in mist. Either Owen is getting taller or I'm sinking.

"You should toss any extra weight."

I drop the blowtorch, which disappears through the mist. Owen motions me toward him.

"You have to keep moving so you don't fall through."

"Fall through what?"

"The cloud. Didn't you want to jump the clouds?" Oh, sweet. Cloud jumping is my absolute favorite pretend activity. I am so liking this dream now.

"Remember, never look down. And try not to miss a cloud, or you'll plunge to your death." He takes off in a run and leaps over to the next cloud. I chase after him. My jump is anything but graceful. The cloud floor is so spongy that my jump has almost no height. I slam smack into the next cloud and thrash my arms around as though I'm caught in quicksand. Owen yanks me up.

"Jump using both feet when you reach the end of the cloud and it will spring up like a diving board. That wasn't too bad for an amateur. At least you didn't look down."

Like an idiot, I look down. We're at airplane height. Farms form a patchwork of green and yellow with tiny red dots for barns. My entire body spasms in fear. Owen tugs me away from the abyss. "We have to keep moving, remember? If you stop, you'll sink through."

I'm about to ask him how we are ever going to get

down from here when he breaks into a run and soars over to the next cloud. I chase after him, remembering to pounce on the end with both feet. The spring takes me clear over him, and I reach the end of the cloud only to spring off that one as well. When I stop thinking about what I'm doing, I find that I can flip, twist, and spin like an Olympic snowboarder. Owen waves when he runs past. I vault over him with a backside triple cork. Apparently, I know how to do that.

We jump cloud after cloud. I don't want to leave, ever. If I never wake up, that's fine by me. Owen and I land at the same time and race across a cloud. We're going to jump together. This will be epic.

Connor appears before us. We screech to a halt, tearing up the mist. "You shouldn't have brought him up here, mate. You know better than that."

"Let him have a night of fun," Owen says.

"He has more important things to do. Return to your forest." Connor flips his hand, and Owen fades away. The kangaroo sets his sights on me. He doesn't even hop, he glides across the cloud. I should be more concerned, but the rush from cloud jumping insulates me. My body throbs with confidence.

"I explained this already," he says. The Australian accent has faded, and his voice sounds more like the echo from earlier. Hold up, could that voice in Echo Forest have been him? Impossible. "You can't keep running away from your problems. We have work to do in the basement."

The basement. I shiver the same way I did in the forest. No, I won't let him drag me there. I back away. Connor glides closer. "Fighting only makes it worse." My confidence wanes. I stop at the edge of the cloud. "You must come with – hey, what do you think you're doing?"

What I'm doing is sinking. The cloud is up to my knees. "This is no time to play around. We have work to do in the basement."

"But the turtles – "

"Yes, the turtles. You must face them. Don't you understand? Nothing will be right until you do." That psycho kangaroo wants to pull me into my nightmare. I'll do anything to get out of it. I'd rather plunge to my death. In three, two, one...

I slip through the cloud. The wind slams against me. I know not to look down this time. Instead, I close my eyes and stretch. The air buffets my back, supporting me. I don't even speed up. Time stretches and folds in upon itself. The blur is comforting, restful.

My eyes open, and I'm back in my room. I never set my alarm on the weekends, but it's the same time I usually get up.

Dad pokes his head in my room. "How are you doing in here?"

"I'm up, OK? I'm up." I'd give anything not be, but I am.

CHAPTER FIFTEEN

As soon as I get my homework out of the way, I'm right back to Orb Quash. After the cave, which is pretty easy for me now, I shoot over the waterfall and navigate the rapids. The twisty stretch at the end always gets me. I'm not convinced it's passable but after only fifty or sixty more tries, I make it through. Turns out, if you complete the rapids, you reach level two where the speed doubles. It's crazy fast. There is no time to react; you have to rely completely on muscle memory.

Dad sits next to me on the couch. "That is crazy fast."

Told ya.

Spears rain down on me, piercing my ball. Now there are spears? I'll have to remember that for next time. Dad covers my phone with his hand before I can restart the game. "I think that's enough Orb Quash."

"Come on, I just started."

"Jake, you've been playing for over an hour. Do something else."

"There's nothing else to do."

"What about your homework?"

"All done. Except for my science presentation, and I'm meeting Jess and Will tomorrow for that."

"Then do something creative. Why don't you draw?" I look at him, cross-eyed. "I'd love to have a new picture to put up in my office," he says.

"I don't feel like drawing anything."

"You used to draw all the time."

"When? When did I draw all the time?" Go on, say it. You know the answer. Before Mom died. We stare at each other, playing a little mental chicken. He blinks first.

"You know, it's a beautiful day. Let's do something outside." Dad leaps off the couch. "To the list."

Did I not mention that he has a list for everything? He keeps the grocery list on the refrigerator and the rest stuffed in a drawer. He sifts through the drawer until he finds the Local Fun List. No kidding, that's the title.

After a brief debate, we choose a park off the list. Dad makes sandwiches while Emma runs upstairs to get her backpack. Not the one she uses for school, mind you. I mean the pint-sized bright pink one. Its sole purpose is to carry Beenie.

On the drive over, Dad turns on his GPS. He knows how to get there – we've hiked the park a million times – but Emma insists on listening to the GPS voice whenever we go anywhere.

Calculating.

Emma squeals with joy. Seriously.

Usually the trail is muddy, but it hasn't rained in over a week. I wish it had. I like to entertain myself by hopping over the mud patches. Now I have to think up another way to pass the time.

"Keep Beenie close," I say. "There are all sorts of wild beasts that eat monkeys around here."

"Daddy?"

"Ignore your brother. There are no jungle cats in Maryland." The twigs crunch under my sneakers. I aim for them.

"Maybe no jungle cats, but there are snakes."

"Daddy?"

"A few little ones. No big snakes like pythons or boa constrictors."

I spring over a log. "That we know of."

"Daddy!"

"Jake, stop tormenting your sister."

Right. Like it's my fault it didn't rain.

Finally, we make it down to the Pop Rocks section. We step across the wet stones until we reach the huge boulders that part the river. After pulling out our lunches, Dad tells us the tale of how the Gunpowder River got its name. I've heard this story before. I'm pretty sure he made it up, but who knows. Dad reads history books. For fun, I mean. Voluntarily.

I finish my sandwich by the time he gets to the good part.

"Our poor hero is about to be hanged," Dad says, "but he convinces the major that he knows where they can find a cache of saltpeter, perhaps enough to turn the tide of the war. He brings the company right here, to the banks of this very river. They're so successful that they decide to grant him a stay of execution."

"Stay?" Emma asks.

"Stay of execution. That means they decide not to kill him. You see, they used saltpeter to make gunpowder and the colonies didn't have much on hand. After they sift through this whole area, they produce so much gunpowder that they're able to sell the extra barrels to the other militias. They make a tidy profit, too. Our hero is saved!"

Emma cheers. She pulls Beenie out of her backpack and dances around the boulder to celebrate. Dad reaches for his camera.

I don't know how Em can be so perky-bubbly-sticky-sweet all the time. She was younger when Mom died; maybe that's why she's so unaffected. All I know is if I have to watch any more of her dopey twirling, I'm going to lose it. I lie down on the boulder and stare up at the sky.

The clouds are wispy today, not optimal for jumping. Whatever. I imagine they're puffier and I'm up there with Mom, teaching her what I learned last night. Jump at the end using both feet. That's it. You've got it.

I close my eyes. Between Emma's laughter and the sun's warmth, I can almost sense Mom's presence beside me.

CHAPTER SIXTEEN

Back at home, Dad changes for his date. The search for Mom's replacement continues. I'm not OK with that. Dad probably knows this by now – it's not like I've been real subtle or anything – but I save my best glare for when he comes downstairs just to be clear.

He frowns. "We're not discussing this again, Jake. When Pau Pau gets here, I expect you to lose the attitude and be nice to her."

"I can't wait until I'm a grown-up," I say. "Then I can do whatever I want."

Dad sighs. "If you actually believe that, you are going to be very disappointed."

Emma squeals excitedly upstairs. She's probably watching the driveway from her window. Sure enough, the doorbell rings. Dad and I let Pau Pau inside.

"Hello, birthday boy!" She spreads her arms. Ugh. I thought we were done with all that birthday stuff. I step forward and let her hug me. She pulls out a red envelope. I take it and look at Dad. "For your birthday," he says.

Emma bounds down the stairs, her Beenie flapping against her back. Pau Pau produces another red envelope. I clear my throat. "Let me help you with the bags," Dad says. "This is a lot of food. You kids are in for a real feast tonight."

"You could stay and help us eat it," I say.

Dad winces. "Have fun with Jake tonight. He's in a real mood."

Dad wasn't kidding about the feast. I eat slowly, partly because I'm using real chopsticks (unlike Emma, who has those kiddy ones fastened by rubber bands) and partly because I need detailed instructions on how to eat this stuff.

Pau Pau likes to say that the Chinese food served in America isn't real Chinese food because Americans' tastes are so different, but I don't think that's the reason. I'm American and this stuff tastes good to me. The problem is that it's so complicated. You'd have to stick a Chinese person at every table just to make sure the food's being eaten correctly.

No, pick it like this from the other end. That's the juiciest part. Wait, pluck out the bone slivers so you don't bleed internally. No, no. Wrong sauce. That one'll blow your head off.

Please. If you can't scoop a handful of grub and cram it directly into your mouth hole, just forget it. This is America: strap on your feedbag and flick on your computer. Don't worry about indigestion. There'll be plenty of pop-up ads for any pill you want.

"Who's ready for dessert?"

I'm ready to explode, but yeah, bring it. Pau Pau sets out every sweet permutation of rice cake, red bean, almond paste, and sugar ever invented over the last millennia behind the Great Wall. And unlike the dinner food, this stuff you can shovel right in. My white half is pleased.

After dinner, we move to the couch. Don't ask me how I get there without a forklift. I try to sit still so my stomach doesn't burst.

I get right back to Orb Quash and figure out how to dodge the spears. The food coma helps; I am creaming this game. Distracting me as always is Emma's dumb giggly show. Or maybe several giggly shows. We sit on the couch for hours.

I may have complained to Dad about Pau Pau being a babysitter, but I really do know the difference. Babysitters, unlike grandparents, follow the parent's rules. Grandparents kinda just do whatever. The three of us veg on the couch well past Emma's bedtime. I have no idea how late it is by the time Pau Pau flicks off the DVR. "Emma's asleep," she says. "You should go to bed, too."

"Yeah, all right." No point arguing. My phone's battery is about to die anyway.

She lifts Em up. "She's so warm and happy all the time. How come you can't be more like your sister?" I'm in a bit of a daze, so I stare at her in response. Did she really just say that?

"Always so mopey. You need to cheer up."

Pau Pau carries Emma up the stairs. I glare at them, but Pau Pau can't see me, so it's not very satisfying. When I look away, I spy Beenie on the couch. Great. One more thing I must do for Emma. I grab her stupid stuffed monkey and stomp up the stairs.

Is Pau Pau serious? I should be more like Emma? Me like her? I stand in the hallway facing Emma's room, clutching Beenie by the neck. My skin tingles with a red-hot rage. Me like her. So, what is she saying? That I shouldn't care about Mom anymore? I should hang out in Emma's weird fantasy world where we pretend everything is wonderful all the time?

Hey, here's an idea. Maybe Emma should be more like me. Did you think of that? Huh? Maybe she should. I stuff Beenie in my closet.

CHAPTER SEVENTEEN

Sitting atop a mound, I survey a grassy field. A familiar prairie dog pops out of a hole near me. We stare at each other while I pull the dream world into focus. I extend my hand. He slaps my palm, calls out with his adorable yippy bark, and zips back into his hole.

That gets me thinking: Em and I have never had any pets. We planned to, back before Mom died.

About a month after Mom's funeral, Dad takes us to the pet store. Emma picks out her fish and cheers each time the sales guy drops a fish he netted into a water-filled baggie. The guy wears gaudy suspenders pinned with a button that reads, *Ask me about our ferrets!* When he finishes, he passes Emma the baggie. She holds it high, poking at whatever fish swim near.

This is our first happy family moment since the funeral, which the sales guy ends in the worst possible way. *If any fish die within a week,* he says, *bring back the dead fish and your receipt, and we'll get you a new fish free of charge.* Emma gasps. Audibly. I mean, everyone in the entire store spins around to gawk. In the awkward silence that follows, I can see Emma's cry develop step by step, like a slow-motion video of a building implosion. First her face contorts, next her body trembles so violently the fish dart against the bag, and finally her piercing wail cuts through the air.

Dad reaches down and peels the baggie from her fingers. She buries her face in his waist while he hands the baggie back to the sales guy. We walk out of there, the three of us, never to return. The fish was for Emma anyway, and it's not like I wanted a ferret. I'm more of a hamster guy. Dad offered to take me back, but I passed when I learned that hamsters live for only two years. We've had our fill of death in this family, thank you very much.

I don't know if thinking about our failed pet-buying attempt caused this, but looking out into the dream world, I have an unexpected urge to visit the basement. Maybe if I can find a way past the turtles, maybe if I can see Mom and talk to her just one more time, then maybe. Maybe I won't be so angry all the time.

Owen comes barreling out of the forest. I'm almost certain the forest has migrated from where it was the last time but whatever. I've learned to let these things go. He flops down next to me. "Connor moved all the portals."

"Oh, no. We can't go cloud jumping?"

"Not if we can't find the portal."

I gaze across the field. "What we need is a GPS."
Owen nudges me with his elbow. Oh, yeah.

GPS.

A GPS appears in my hands. Sweet. I flick the thing
on.

State your destination.

"Portal to the clouds."

Calculating. She sounds just like Dad's GPS.

"Why do they always say 'calculating'? This isn't a
math problem. They should say, 'Chill for a sec while I map
this out,' you know?"

Owen shrugs. "Technology for an orangutan is
finding the perfect stick."

Right. I think I may be on my own here.

*Route complete. Walk twenty yards and turn left
onto the orange path.*

We follow her directions. Don't ask me where this
orange path comes from. We were on a prairie a moment
ago.

*Continue ten yards to the fork in the road and take
the mauve path.*

Owen and I come to a full stop. The path branches
in at least thirteen different directions, each marked with a
different shade of purple.

"You gotta be kidding me. Which one is mauve?"

"Mauve." Owen squints. "That's a type of
rhinoceros?"

Yeah, I'm definitely on my own here. I try the first
path. We don't get too far.

*Recalculating. Make a U-turn, double back on the
lavender path, and take the mauve path.*

We head back to the fork and take the next path.

Recalculating. Make a U-turn, double back on the magenta path, and take the mauve path.

We return to the fork and try a few more paths. Every time is the same.

Recalculating...

I reconsider my plan. At this rate, I'll be here all night. I'm liable to wake up before I get anywhere. I glare at the path colors. Who could possibly need this many shades of purple?

"Let's choose a path and stay on it," I say. "Maybe we'll figure something out later."

We set out on another path. I stare at the GPS. For once, she's silent.

"Hey, maybe we guessed right."

Recalculating.

"Oh, for crying out – "

Make a U-turn, double back on the indigo path, and take the mauve path.

"Yeah, not going to happen."

We continue walking. I am such a rebel.

Recalculating.

"Forget it."

Recalculating.

"You do whatever you want. I'm in an indigo mood."

The GPS sighs.

"Hold up, did you just sigh?"

Sometimes I wonder why I even bother.

"I'm...I'm sorry. I don't know what mauve looks like. If you'd give me better directions – "

You're saying this is my fault?

"No, but, I mean...Owen, help me out here."

"My stick never talks back."

Yes. Helpful. Thanks.

"Can't we just continue down this path?" I ask the GPS.

Sure, if you want to go the wrong way.

"Wow. You're a snippy GPS, aren't you?"

My name isn't Snippy.

Not the answer I expected. Then again, I've never chatted with a GPS before.

"I didn't know you had a name."

Why wouldn't I have a name? Don't you have a name?

"Sure, but I'm—" I cut myself off. "OK, so what's your name?"

Ginny.

"Ginny the GPS?"

I prefer Ginny. Unless you want me to call you Jacob the person.

"No, just Jake is fine."

OK, Just Jake. I need you to follow my directions, so we can get out of here. You've taken us into The Land of Do the Opposite of Your Gut Instinct. Since I have no guts, this place confuses me.

"Do the opposite of your gut instinct? If I do that, I'll have to stop talking to a box."

A girl walks toward me. "Then that's what you should do."

CHAPTER EIGHTEEN

The girl's voice is identical to Ginny's, but that isn't what startles me. It's that she's a girl, an actual person, in my dream. I can't remember the last time a human showed up in my dream.

She puts her hands on her hips. "Why were you talking into that thing, anyway?"

"Because your voice was coming out of it."

"My voice is also coming out of this," she says, pointing to her mouth.

Now that she's directed my attention to her mouth, I realize that it's awfully pretty. Her lips glisten in the moonlight. She's like a cross between a GPS and, well, Jess. She wears boxy black pants and a boxy black leather jacket. Her hair is braided into a cube shape. As absurd as all that sounds, she's rocking the look. I get shy like I always do around cute girls and stammer. She cuts me off.

"If you had followed my directions, we'd be there already. You refuse to let other people help you. Why is that? What are you afraid of?"

"I'm not afraid of anything."

"Or maybe you're afraid of *everything*."

"Um, I think that's a stretch."

"Yes. It's important to stretch before physical activity. I assume you're about to run." She backs away, distracted by a presence behind me.

"Why would you assume that?"

"You're not? Oh, well, I guess you aren't afraid of everything. Most people run when a giant bazookapus is bearing down on them."

Owen clambers up a tree. These two must be reacting to something scary. More than anything, I want to turn around, so I don't. I find it oddly refreshing to do the opposite of my gut instinct.

"What the heck is a bazookapus?" I say.

"The thing bearing down on you. Don't you ever listen?"

"No, I mean, what's it like?"

"Flowers, but there's no time to buy them now."

Ugh. I can't even get frustrated with her. This is my dream.

The pounding behind me increases in intensity, shaking the ground with every thud. My gut screams at me to run, but I stay put. I wish I could be this brave outside my dreams.

I hear a snarfing sound followed by a hot air gust against my neck. I reach behind me. The creature has downy soft fur. The last thing I want to do is look into its eyes. Drat. I look into its eyes.

The brontosaurus-sized monster is matted with thick green hair that covers its entire body except for its strikingly white eyebrows. Its tail wags when I stroke its fur, swatting trees with each swipe. Guess I found a pet after all.

Ginny inches toward me. "Why would you pet him?"

"Like you said. I didn't have time to buy flowers."

She nods. "That makes sense."

Sure it does.

"Can you get us out of here?" I ask her.

"Yes. Chill for a sec while I map this out."

"Wait, did you just say –"

"Oh, what? I have to say 'recalculating'? Is that want you want?"

"No, it's that –"

"I am sick of everyone trying to put me in a box. Have you ever felt that way? Like you're stuck in a box and can't get out?"

"Can't say I have."

"Huh, I thought you could relate."

"Not really." I lift the GPS unit with the hand not still petting the bazookapus. "I don't live in a box."

"Don't be so sure. There are all kinds of boxes. When people see you in a certain way, it's difficult to get them to realize there's more to you than that. You wind up buying into it and acting the way they expect you to. I think you've been stuck in a box for a long time."

She takes the GPS unit from me and stuffs it in her pocket. "In my box, I'm expected to give directions, to be sure where I want to go. Mostly I do know, but not always. I can be as lost as anybody. There's much more to me than people will accept. People want us to stay in our boxes because it's easier to think of us as only one thing. But why do I have to be what others want me to be?"

I understand what she means. The way some people see me and the way I see myself doesn't always match up. I'd hate to do that to her. "OK," I say. "If you could do anything you wanted, what would it be?"

"I'd love to paint."

"Paint?"

"Or sculpt maybe. Just create art. I am so tired of always coming up with the most direct way to do things. I want to explore. I want to dance."

"Huh. I would not have guessed that."

Her smile collapses. "Recalculating."

"What? Oh, I get it. I'm putting you in a box, right? No, you go ahead and explore. We can find the portal to the clouds another time. Cloud jumping is a blast, though. You might enjoy it."

Her smile returns. "You want me to join you?"

"Sure. Right, Owen?"

He swings from the branches above, working his way down to join us.

"Oh, wonderful," she says. "In that case, the red portal is right there."

And so it is. Straight up the path.

"Hey, I thought only the mauve path would take us there."

"Don't be such a stickler," she says. "Purple is purple."

We wave goodbye to the friendly neighborhood bazookapus and race toward the portal. When we jump through, the purple paths vanish, but no sky appears. Instead, I slam into a door. Beside it stands Connor, his arms folded, his tail thumping impatiently.

"Time to enter the basement, mate. You've put this off for far too long."

CHAPTER NINETEEN

Connor is surrounded by a mob of kangaroos. Owen and Ginny stand beside me.

"You again!" Owen glares at Connor and hyperventilates through pursed lips, producing a squeaky kissing sound. "You're like a bad vegetable. You always turn up."

"Now hold on," Conner says. "A turnip is not a bad vegetable. If you sauté it with olive oil, it's quite tasty. You could say I'm like a root vegetable. I'd give you that."

"You can keep it. I'd never root for a vegetable."

Connor blinks hard and curls his ears as if he's bitten into a sour jaw-breaker. "You're an odd bloke. Enough of you." He flicks his hand and Owen vanishes. Next, he looks Ginny over and scoffs. "I see someone's escaped her box."

"Wait," I say, but it's too late. Ginny transforms into a tornado of ones and zeros before blasting inside the GPS unit. Connor catches the box in his hand and flips it to another kangaroo, who drops it into her pouch. A joey pops his head out and pokes at the box like it's his new smartphone.

"I wish you wouldn't do that to my friends."

"No worries. They'll be back later. It's time to enter the basement. Everyone's waiting for you."

I wonder who everyone is. Mom? I want to try, but my gut tells me to run, get away, do something, anything else. In my panic, I forget to ignore it, and I race back to the portal. I don't get far – iron bars slam down around me. This is so unfair. I glare at Connor and swing my hand. The bars rattle. Whoa. I swing my hand wider and the bars rip out of the ground and disappear into the night.

Connor's ears shoot up. "Don't do this. Fighting only makes it worse." More iron bars slam down around me. I brush those away only to get caught behind another set of iron bars and another and another. He's way too fast for me to keep up. Now the iron bars have iron bars.

That's a bit silly, even for one of my dreams. I wonder how much untapped power I have in here. Instead of trying to brush the bars away, I extend my hands and push with all my strength.

I find myself standing in an empty room. On a screen before me is a projection of my dream. The kangaroos, the iron bars, the basement door – everything – is two-dimensional. I tap the screen. The image vibrates like ripples in a stagnant pond, flipping the kangaroos into the air like in Orb Quash. Sweet.

The kangaroos punch, kick, and hop into the screen but cannot get through. While they fail, I succeed in knocking over every one of them. I'm pretty smug about this until I realize Connor is standing next to me.

He strikes a devilish grin. "Have you figured out who I am?"

"You're freaking me out."

"No. Well maybe, but that's not who I am."

"You're my greatest nemesis."

Connor throws his head back when he laughs. "No, not that either, although I will be if you don't stop messing with your dreams. This is your last warning."

"It's only a dream," I say. "What difference does it make?"

I mean really. None of this is real. What could he do to me?

"Dreams are important, Jake. You need to stop interfering."

"I don't need to stop. I need to figure this out."

I pull myself out of the dream and sit up in my bed. What time is it? My vision is so blurry I can't make out the numbers on my clock. Guess I'll get up anyway; it's not like I'm going back to sleep. Was last night Saturday or Sunday? I can't remember if today's a school day.

"Dad?" No answer. The morning is overcast. The air in my room appears as hazy as my brain. I tug my shirt on, but I must have stuck my head in the wrong opening because now I'm caught in my shirt. I struggle with the thing until I decide the pull it off. When I do, I see movement by my closet. I freeze in place. I must be wrong, but it sure looked like a kangaroo.

Great. Now I'm hallucinating.

I see something shift on my bed, and I swing around. Nothing. Take it easy, Jake. I rotate my shirt in my hands, unable to decipher the thing. Why are there so many holes in this shirt? Forget it. I'll get a different shirt. I spot activity again, this time by my door. When I turn, I see nothing unusual.

An eerie dread surges through my body. "Dad, are you up?"

A voice from behind me says, "He can't help you, mate."

I spin around in time to see Conner hammer-fist my skull. A sharp pain causes me to collapse onto the floor. It hurts. Like real searing pain. I reach up and touch something wet. Wait, am I bleeding? Did I wake up, or didn't I?

The kangaroo mob hovers over me. "What the hell is happening?"

Conner lowers his face to the carpet. "Why even ask? You never listen until it's too late, and then it's too late to listen."

Kangaroos pounce over me. I thrash on the ground to protect my head. The room begins to spin on an oblique axis, twirling faster and faster. I dig my nails into the carpet to keep from flying off. I know my room can't actually be spinning, but the nausea is real. I must still be dreaming. Hold up. If I can bleed here, does that mean I can die?

"Dad. Mom? Anybody!"

Connor is in my face again. "We cry out for help, but what would help is to cry."

Make him stop. Please.

"We think 'stop,' yet we never stop to think."

Stop? Think? I'm too confused to do anything more than claw the carpet. A voice calls my name. It's muffled at first, then clearer. "Jake?"

Dad? How is he here? So, wait, this isn't a dream? I can't tell what's real anymore.

"Jake!"

The room contracts into my skull. I blink, and everything is peaceful, still. The morning sun streams through my window. So much for it being overcast. Dad rushes over and lifts my head. When I move, the carpet brushes against my fingertips. "Where am I?"

"In your room. You fell out of bed. Ouch, looks like you banged your head. You're bleeding."

"Am I going to die?"

"No, I don't think so. You just need a Band-Aid." He helps me sit up. "That must have been some vivid dream." That's Dad, the King of Understatement. Whatever. It's not like I could explain this. It's not like he'd ever believe me even if I could.

Dad brushes my hair away from the cut on my forehead. "When you're ready to talk," he says, curling his lips into a sad smile. "I'm ready to listen."

CHAPTER TWENTY

That morning, Emma flips out. Dad had just finished bandaging my cut when we hear her shriek. Startled, we exchange glances and race from the bathroom to see what's wrong. I'm not really that talented an actor - I had simply forgotten why she'd be upset. "I can't find Beenie!" Then I remember.

We enter Emma's room. The place hasn't changed in years. As always, it gives me a raging pink headache. Her room is cutesy with a capital Kewpie doll, sparkly and chaotic as if a glitter tornado tore through. And that was true even before she stripped her bed.

"Beenie is missing. I can't find her anywhere." Emma holds her blanket in one hand and the sheets in the other. She paces around, dragging everything behind her. She's gone ballistic, berserk, bananas. Actually that last one works best.

Emma has gone bananas.

"Beenie!" Emma darts into the hallway, screaming at the top of her lungs. Her stuffed monkey does not respond.

I figure I'm on my own for breakfast. I head into the kitchen and pop frozen waffles in the toaster. Even after I finish eating, Emma and Dad are still on their monkey hunt. Well, no need for this morning to be a total bust. I move to the couch and play Orb Quash.

"Jake."

"Hang on a sec."

"Jake, turn that off."

Dad messes up my timing and I die. I didn't even reach stage two. "Yeah?"

"No games until we find Beenie."

"What? How is this my fault?" Dad sits next to me. "No one said it's your fault, but we're not doing anything else until we find Beenie. We're a family."

More like the remains of a family, the hollow shell of a family. Let's see, there's me, Dad, Emma, and that neglected ghost, Mom, the spectral elephant in the room. I can't even remember the last time we talked about Mom as a family. Hold up, I remember. Last year Dad asked Em and me if we thought it was time to take down the wedding photo framed on the living room wall. We both said no. That was the entire conversation.

"Maybe it's OK that we can't find Beenie," I say. "Those two can use a break."

"No. We need to find her." Dad seems to be missing the opportunity here.

"Don't you think Emma's too obsessed with that thing?"

He settles against the couch cushion, rubbing his temples. "It's more complicated than that. Trust me."

Emma clomps up the stairs and stands before us. She tugs at her rainbow pajamas, scrunching them in her fists. She looks how I feel every morning. It's not so bad to have company. I don't mean to be callous, but not having to deal with her drippy sweet nonsense for a whole morning is a major relief. "Think, honey," Dad says. "When did you see her last?" Emma squinches her eyes and seizes the back of her head. We stare for several seconds. Finally, Dad turns to me. "When did *you* see her last?"

I squirm. "Emma had her all night."

"Pau Pau," Emma says. Her eyes flash open. "Maybe Pau Pau put her somewhere?"

Dad stands up. "I doubt it, but I'll give her a call. Jake, help your sister search."

I grumble. Everything falls to me around here. Emma pleads with her brown eyes, just irritating me further. Oh, you want my help? Fine.

"Monkeys like to climb things. Have you checked the ceilings?"

Emma gasps. "No, I haven't."

"We should start –" She zips up the stairs.

Guess we'll start upstairs. We check the ceiling of each room and hallway in the house. We live in a split level, so we check all three bedrooms and the bathroom, go down the stairs to the kitchen and living room, and go down the rest of the stairs to the foyer, den, and the small bathroom.

No sign of Beenie. As much as I hate to admit it, it's kinda fun. We dash from room to room like hyper Golden Retriever pups, double- and triple-checking each space, shouting "Clear!" whenever we leave a room. We even grab the bananas on the way downstairs. You know, for bribing purposes.

"Come out, come out, wherever you are." I croon my words like an old-time singer. "These yummy, ripe bananas are all for you." Emma giggles and wipes her tears. For a moment, I regret causing all this trouble. I'm about to tell her where Beenie is – really, I swear – but then she says this:

"Maybe Beenie's in the basement." That stops me cold.

"We have to go down there." She tugs my hand.

I yank it away. "I don't want to."

"Come on." She reaches for my hand, but I'm too quick this time.

"You go ahead. I'm staying here." Emma's dimples deepen. She shakes her head the way Mom used to, a gesture that means I'm not angry, just disappointed. She looks an awful lot like Mom.

"Why don't you ever play in the basement anymore?"

My anger swells like a fire, blackening and twisting my innards. Words spray from my mouth like venom. "Why do I have to go to the stupid basement? Why would Beenie even be down there? Maybe she left. Huh, did you think of that? Maybe she got tired of hanging around your neck all the time. Maybe she grew up and ran away!"

Dad rushes downstairs during my outburst, and I thrust the bananas at his chest before sprinting up the stairs. I slam the door, dive onto my bed, and strangle the pillow.

I hate being this angry. It scares me. Even more than Brandon. Even more than Connor. Even more than losing the rest of my family.

CHAPTER TWENTY-ONE

At lunchtime, Dad calls me downstairs. Apologies are exchanged all around. Dad relieves me of all future monkey-hunt responsibilities and Emma says she's sorry for being so bossy. For my part, I swear up and down that I do not really believe Beenie ran away because she didn't want to hang out with Emma anymore.

I don't know why it bothers me that Emma still acts like she's four. Let her be a baby forever. When I go off to college, Dad can pour her milk. Not my problem.

After lunch, I stuff my science notes into my backpack, tear off my Band-Aid, and walk my bicycle out of the garage. I haven't been to Jess's house in years and I've never biked there, but I'm not worried. Jess gave us directions on Friday. Will wrote them down since he's new to the area. I didn't need to.

I ride for what seems longer than necessary. I'm almost positive she told us to take Superior Avenue to Erie Avenue and make the next right to reach Ontario Avenue, but I get my Great Lakes mixed up sometimes. When I stop to read a street sign, I realize I'm on Placid Avenue. I suppose I'm in the right neighborhood since that's also a lake name.

I backtrack to Erie Avenue and loop around. Thankfully, that route also leads me to Ontario Avenue. I count the house numbers until I see Jessica's dad waving from the porch.

"We were worried about you, Jake. I thought you got trapped in the falls."

I drop my bike by the garage and walk toward the house.

"You know, Niagara Falls," he says. "Between Lake Erie and Lake Ontario."

"Yeah, I got it."

He shakes my hand. Why do grown-ups always do that? I'm not here for a business meeting. Now that I see him up close, he reminds me a little of my own dad. Similar earnest eyebrows, similar amiable smile. His shirt isn't wrinkled, though. I feel kinda bad blowing off his dumb joke, so I offer a dumb joke of my own.

"On the way over here, I stopped by Lake Placid for a little water skiing."

He finds this hysterical. Adults are so easy to entertain.

"No wonder you're late. You missed the turn if you went that far." Still chuckling, he walks me in. "Jessica. Jake's here."

I follow the sound of talking to her room. She and Will are sitting on the floor with a laptop between them. Jess frowns when I enter.

"Really, Jake. You couldn't follow my directions? What, what's so funny?"

Nothing, Ginny. "Your dad and I were joking around."

"And he was actually funny?"

"Uh, in the same goofy way my dad can be funny." She seems to buy that. I sit in front of the laptop.

"Catch me up."

"We found a whole bunch of information on logging and palm oil plantations, the main causes of deforestation in Sumatra," Will says. "We haven't come up with any solutions yet."

"That shouldn't be hard to find. Go back to the search engine page. Whoa. What the heck is that?"

"DuckDuckGo." Will points to the screen and reads, "The search engine that doesn't track you."

"Track us? Who would track us?"

"You know, the government. The NSA." Will glances from me to Jess. "They gather information on everybody and store it on huge databases in the desert."

I wait for the punchline, but there isn't any.

"And in Maryland, by the way," he adds.

"Do you know how crazy you sound?"

"I'm serious," Will says. "It was in the news. I'm not making this up."

I look at Jess. She shrugs.

"I think you like this site because there's a duck on it," I say. "You've got this weird thing with ducks."

"If it searches like a duck."

"Exactly. OK, have your duck search orangutan deforestation."

He types it in and scrolls down the list. Will and I click the YouTube link. Jess takes notes the whole time, but I think she'd be better off watching. It's the visual that's brutal.

The video opens with trucks hauling away hundreds of cut trees. We see a massive clear-cut area dotted by knee-high palm oil plants. Next, cranes tear at the edge of a lush forest. The scene cuts to vast devastation after a forest fire. Through the smoky haze, only a few spindly trees in the background are left standing. The camera focuses on a ditch where a single orangutan wanders through the desolation. The poor guy appears lost, like he's the lone survivor in a post-apocalyptic movie. Since orangutans rely on the forest to survive, that's basically true for him.

"This is disturbing," Jess says, glancing at her notes. "Palm oil is found in forty percent of supermarket products and it's rarely labeled. And even when it is, there's no way to know if it's *sustainable* palm oil. We're all contributing to the problem, and we don't even realize it. It's so frustrating." She slams her notes on the carpet. "I'll be right back."

"What's wrong?"

"Nothing's wrong, I'm just going to the bathroom." She scampers out of the room. "Keep working without me."

"Guess she really had to go," Will says.

"Yeah. Go back to the search list." I take off my glasses and rub my nose. I have lightweight frames, but they still get heavy after a while.

"Hey, stick these over there for me so I don't sit on them." Will places my glasses next to a pack of strawberry gum on Jess's desk. Oh yeah, strawberry. I guess it wasn't her shampoo I smelled.

"There are too many sites," Will says. "This'll take all day."

"Let's get real. We're not going to think up a solution by tomorrow. Which of these sites do you think has done the most work for us already? Oh, right there. Click on the link to the World Wildlife Federation."

We hit the mother lode. When Jess gets back, we write up the entire presentation on PowerPoint. Here's our plan: Jess opens with details of the problem, Will segues into a list of solutions, and I end with the consequences of inaction on endangered wildlife.

While Will and Jess work out the final details, I scroll through YouTube. "Oh, here's another video on Sumatra. This looks unsettling."

"No," Jess says. "No more videos. I'm sick of the videos." Her annoyed tone irritates me. Are we so busy I can't watch a video? "We finished the work. It's not like I'm wasting time. What's the problem?"

"That's not - forget it. Go ahead and watch if you want."

Jess and I share an awkward silence until Will stands. "I'm gonna go," he says. "I think our presentation is solid. I'll review this tonight."

"Yeah, I guess I'll head out, too," I say. "Don't worry, Jess. I'll have it all down."

Jess stares at her carpet. "I'm sure you will. Thanks for coming, guys."

Downstairs, we see Jess's parents on the couch. They're holding hands and laughing. It's been a long time since I saw that scene in my house.

"Bye," Will says. "Thanks for having us over."

"Yeah," I say.

Jess's mom walks us out. I go to fix my glasses and end up whacking myself in the face. "Oh, shoot," I tell her. "I left my glasses upstairs."

I walk up to Jess's room. Outside her door, I hear a faint whimper. When I push the door open, a startled Jess rubs her face. She is sitting on her bed, her cheeks streaked with tears. "What's wrong?" I say.

I can tell she's about to deny everything, so I gesture for her to wait. I cross the room and sit next to her. She takes a few deep breaths and slumps to the side. "I keep picturing orangutans burning up in the forest. It's too horrible. This whole thing is more than I can – " She slaps her thighs and straightens up. "It's fine. I'll be fine."

"You don't have to be."

She freezes in place. "It's OK, Jess. Really. You don't have to act so strong all the time. I mean, I know you are, but you don't always have to act it. Not with me. You can be whatever you want with me." Jess blinks. I cannot read her expression at all. Maybe I upset her again, I don't know. I seem to do that a lot these days.

She rests her head on my shoulder and wraps her arm around me, cloaking me with warmth.

I hold still. I barely even breathe. I have no idea what I'm supposed to do. I wouldn't mind putting my arm around her, but I'm afraid if I move at all, she'll pull away. I should do something, though. Think. Ugh, I'm screwing this up, I just know it. What are the rules here? Girls should really come with a manual. This stuff is complicated.

She sits up and smiles. Her hand rests on the nape of my neck until she presses her fingers into my hair. "Your hair is smooth and spiky." She runs her hand through my hair and looks away shyly. "I guess you think I'm weird that want to touch your hair."

"Um...no. Not really."

I smile back. She is still petting my hair. Before I even realize what I'm doing, I reach out and touch her neck. Her skin is soft and smooth until I reach her hair. My fingers loop around a braid and the knots bump against my fingertips. Our faces move closer until I can feel her breath on my lips.

"Did you find your glasses?"

Jess and I pull away from each other. Jess's mom looms in the doorway. She appears both surprised and amused, a combination I don't think I've ever seen before. Hold up, yes, I have. I watched this nature documentary once where a lioness happens upon her prey unexpectedly. That's the same expression she flashes the moment before an easy meal. "I haven't looked yet," I say. "We got distracted."

"I noticed." My body flushes. What exactly did she notice?

I turn to Jess. "I left my glasses on your desk."

She reaches for my glasses and hands them to me. I put them on. The room pulls into focus, but I still can't see my way out of this situation.

"I should go," I say.

"Sure you don't want to stay for dinner?"

"Mom!"

I stand. "No. Thanks." No one moves. I fix my glasses. "I should go." Jess's mom steps aside, and I bolt out of there.

Back on the road, I stomp my bike pedals as hard as I can. I'm not in a rush; I just need to blow off extra steam. My house seems much closer on the trip home, so I shoot by it and take a few laps around the neighborhood. That doesn't help much.

I pull into my driveway, breathless and sweaty. A cold shower helps a bit. At dinner, I have an unusually good appetite. Dad finds this amusing and makes a comment about how his growing boy is fast becoming a man. Really not helping, Dad.

CHAPTER TWENTY-TWO

By the time I settle in for bed, I'm able to relax. Along with my agitation, the whole experience has faded like a hazy dream. Wait, did I dream that? No. My shoulder still tingles from where Jess touched me.

Unfortunately, the shoulder tingling reminds me of Brandon. And my stay of execution, which expires in the morning.

Great, tomorrow I have to confront a bully twice my size and a friend I nearly kissed. As usual, I haven't the faintest idea how to handle either situation.

Dad knocks on my door and enters the room. "OK in here?"

"Yep," I say.

He rests against my closet. "Getting Emma down

was tough tonight. I had to let her hold me for almost an hour. I think I fell asleep part of the time."

Yeah, that's one more thing I don't want to deal with right now.

"Something on your mind?"

I'm about to answer no. Instinct, I guess. But then I figure, I don't know, maybe he can help.

"Have you ever had a problem that seems so complicated, no matter how hard you look at it, you still can't see the answer?"

Dad takes a deep breath and releases it slowly. "Come over to the window."

I walk over to the window. Dad flicks off the light.

"I want you to look at the brightest star up there. Look right at it, then a little off to the side, and then right at it again." I do what he says. Then I do it again because what just happened could not have happened.

"Whoa."

"Cool, right? What did you see?"

"The star vanished when I looked right at it but when I looked a little off to the side, it came back."

"Exactly. Life can be like that. You can stare at a problem forever and never see the answer, but when you look a little off to the side? There it is. And like with the stars, the answer was there the whole time, staring you in the face."

We gaze at the stars together.

"That is cool," I say. "Not really helpful, but still cool."

He kisses the top of my head. "You sleep on it. And if you want me to be more helpful, you might want to tell me exactly what's going on in your brain."

"Yeah, no, I'm just joking. That was helpful. Thanks, Dad."

After he leaves, I crawl into bed. I don't want to think about Brandon or even Jess. I'm too worked up to think about Mom. Instead, I think about Connor.

He and I need to talk. And by talk, I mean have it out. And by have it out, I mean an epic battle where only one of us is left standing. So not really talk at all.

Maybe I should start over.

Nah, forget it, time to dream. Come and get me, Connor. You know where to find me.

CHAPTER TWENTY-THREE

When I enter the dream world, I see no sign of Connor. Still, I'm wary. He could spring into action at any moment.

I seem to be wandering through a street fair. Animals hawk their merchandise: pre-owned underwear (don't touch the yellow parts), toilet thrones (for porcelain royalty), spiral UFO detectors (as if I need this dream to get weirder), marbles shaped like the presidents (the William Taft marble rolls), and collector airline bags. I don't check to see if the bags are pre-owned, but they have a barfy smell so I'm thinking yes.

This dream is odd even for me. Bizarre, one could say. Yes, a bizarre bazaar. Knowing my brain, that must be where I was going with this. OK, time to do my thing.

I sharpen my focus, deepening the colors.

GINNY THE GPS.

Ginny appears, black box in hand.

"Have you figured out the portal situation?" I ask her.

Ginny frowns. "Don't you say hello? You should get some manners."

"I could. The dung beetles are selling manners over at table forty-three."

She closes her eyes. "Calculating." Her eyes flash open. "So they are. We'll stop by later. First we have a problem to solve."

She takes off through the small mammal sector. I jog after her. Considering how un-aerodynamic Ginny is, she moves at a remarkable clip. When I catch up, I find her standing in front of a red door. "See how much faster it goes when you follow my direction?"

Maybe I *should* call her Snippy.

"One slight problem though." She motions for me to try the doorknob. It won't budge.

"Connor must have locked the portal," I say. "No problem, I'll just conjure up a key." RED KEY. I try my red key, but it isn't even remotely the right size. It's like trying to stick an elephant in a shoe box.

"That's a fail."

Don't worry," Ginny says. "There's a key store behind us."

"Come on. There's no such thing as a –" I see the key store behind us. Of course there's a key store behind us. Why had I doubted her?

Ginny leads me by the arm. We approach a table where a porcupine brushes her bristles. Her table is empty, but I ask anyway.

"Do you have a key to the red door?"

"I can't help you," she says. She lifts her fingers above her head. Her mouth opens impossibly wide, and she vomits a pile of goopy hands. They thump onto the table and wiggle around. "I'm afraid I've thrown up my hands."

"Literally," I say.

"Psst."

We swing around. A hulking creature lumbers out of the shadows. He's a bull with bulging biceps, colossal calves, devastating deltoids, erratic eyebrows, fierce forearms, gigantic guts, humongous hips, immense...OK, you get the idea. Let's just say he's really big.

"You seek the red key," he says. When he huffs, steam rattles past the ring in his nose. "Follow me."

"I don't trust him," Ginny whispers.

I don't either, but I still find myself following. I worry I'm losing control. Something familiar about the bull blocks my ability to use my brain. A clammy sweat bristles across my skin. Anxiety compels me to comply.

"It's right over there." The bull points his knobby arm.

When I step around him to look, he shoves me onto the ground. A pack of hands ambush me like starved piranhas, tugging me in all directions, pinching and scratching. The bull snickers. "You've played right into my hands."

I swat away the hands that try to latch on to my face, but like when I battled the foot swarm a few nights ago, using force gets me nowhere.

"You're no match for me." The bull releases another haughty snort.

I recognize the sound and his dumb stare. How could I not? He's Brandon the bull.

"I can beat you with one hand tied behind my back." The bull spins around to show me the hand tied behind his back. The hand bows, jangling a red key from its fingertips.

Ginny brightens. "The key is close at hand."

I refocus to gain control over my body. The hands keep poking at me, but I ignore them and think. I must beat him at his own game. Oh, I know.

I yank two grabby hands and stack them on the floor. I do the same to the next pair, and the next, until I've created a tower of hands.

The bull snorts. "What do you think you're doing?"

I seize the hand on top. "Now *I've* got the upper hand. You should never have shown me the key – you tipped your hand. And now I'm going to tip the rest of them."

I give the stack a shove, and the hands crash onto the floor. Their fingers writhe in the air like capsized beetles.

"I've won hands down," I say. "Now hand it over."

The bull sulks. "I've got to hand it to you," he says, untying the hand behind his back.

I snatch the key from its fingers and make for the portal, beckoning Ginny. "Let's get out of here before we're arrested by the Pun Police."

"There are Pun Police?"

Oops. I should not have said that. Behind us, the Pun Police race forward, shaking their batons. I jiggle the key into the slot, but the lock is sticky. The Pun Police close in fast. We're running out of time.

I swing around to face the crowd. "Who here wants us to make it? Let's see a show of hands."

And with that, the hands swarm the Pun Police. Some dance, others perform handstands. A chorus sings what I can only assume to be Handel's *Messiah*. All told, they put on quite a show.

With the Pun Police distracted, Ginny and I slip through the portal.

CHAPTER TWENTY-FOUR

Surrounded by blue sky, Ginny and I stand on a familiar mist. "Keep walking so you don't slip through," I say.

Ginny spins around. "Are we really on a cloud?" We are. She led me to the right portal this time. I figure Connor will show up at any moment, so I waste no time.

"Be sure to jump using both feet when you reach the end of the cloud. Let's go."

We race the length of the cloud hand in hand. A cool wind swirls through my hair, invigorating me. We pounce when we reach the end only to smack into a clear wall like a fly on the windshield. A squeaking noise accompanies our slide down.

When I'm able to stand, I find Conner by the portal door. He cringes.

"Sorry, mate. I didn't think you'd jump that hard into

it. But I did know you'd come here. Next time you want to dodge somebody, don't be so predictable. And by the way, the glass slopes under the cloud. You won't be slipping away this time."

I brush myself off and assume the ninja fighting position.

"Relax. I'm not here to spar. I have news. It's about your mother."

"What about her?"

"I did a little investigation and it turns out you're right. She is here."

I relax my stance. "In the basement?"

"That's not for me to say, but you will have to get through the basement before you can see her. I will take you there if you're willing to go." I look from Connor to Ginny.

"Ginny won't be able to help you," Conner says. "You must do this on your own." My sinking feet settle against the glass floor. I kick at the cloud. I'm stuck, but I always have been. Night after night, I end up in the same place.

"Take me to the basement."

We're there in a blink. The breeze is replaced by stagnant air heavy with a moldy funk. I rest my hand on the basement door. Cold tremors vibrate down my arm. "I don't know if I can do this," I say.

"You're not afraid of me or the bazookapus, yet a few turtles make you doubt yourself? Why is that?"

"I don't know."

"You do know because I know," Connor says. "You've chosen to forget, but I have no choice but to remember."

"Connor, seriously, can you stop talking in riddles?

You're hard to follow."

"Yes, we can be like that at times."

We who? Are there more psychotic kangaroos I haven't met?

"I am neither psychotic nor a kangaroo," Connor says. "Who am I?"

Someone who needs to stop reading my mind.

"Let's focus on the turtles," I say. "I'd rather tackle one impossible problem at a time."

"There is no impossible. Only a probable lack of imagination."

I squint at him. "Seriously, quit it. And why does your accent go away whenever you talk in riddles?"

"Dunno mate. Why is that?"

Yeah, I'm overthinking this again.

When I focus on the basement door, my fear rushes back, overpowering and – Connor is right – completely out of proportion. And it isn't just my fear that consumes me; there's something else. Something irrational. Fury. Rage. An explosive anger.

"That's where you keep it," Connor says. "You push it all down here, but it will not be contained. It seeps into the waking world, gaining strength night after night. And it will grow ever more powerful until you choose to stop it."

"Then I choose to stop it."

"Do you?"

"Well, yes. I just said so."

"Words have no meaning here. Only actions count."

"Fine. I'll tear those turtles apart."

Connor frowns. "You cannot beat anger with more anger."

"Watch me."

I fling the door open, but I find no turtles, only a flaming orb, throbbing in the darkness. I lift my fists and yell. The orb bursts into an inferno that surges up the stairs and blasts into me. The energy flattens me onto my back, searing into my eyes, plunging down my throat to vaporize my scream.

I wake up in bed unable to speak or breathe. The light continues to scorch my eyes. Helpless, I relax my anger. The glow fades into darkness.

I sit up. The numbers on my digital clock glow 2:07. I reach back and touch my damp pillow.

Guess I lost. Again.

After flipping the pillow to the dry side, I lie back down. Eventually I fall asleep, but I don't even try to remember any more dreams. The night slips away until my alarm buzzes me awake.

Time for school. One more impossible problem followed by another.

CHAPTER TWENTY-FIVE

When Emma comes downstairs for breakfast, I hold out the Elmo bowl. She stares at it for a moment and pushes it away.

"I want a regular bowl," she says.

I swap it out with a bowl that matches mine. She drifts over to the table. I try not to stare but I find it odd to see her so restrained, or without a stuffed monkey around her neck.

I sit next to her and pour my cereal. When I pass her the box, she pours her own cereal. Some of it spills out of her bowl but still, I've never seen her try before. She scoops up the wayward flakes while I pour my milk. Just to see what'll happen, I pass her the milk.

She stares at it. Then she pours her own milk. She does a good job until her hand dips and the milk shoots off the side of her bowl. The milk streams to the table's edge and dribbles onto the floor. Emma stares at the mess. Her eyes well with tears.

"No big deal," I say. "Easy to clean up."

I get the paper towels off the counter and hand her a bunch. After I staunch the dripping, I drop a few towels onto the puddle by my feet. For her part, Emma holds the towels and cries.

"You know the saying, don't cry over spilled milk?" I say.

"Uh-huh."

"It's actually not a saying; it's a rule. You're not *allowed* to cry over spilled milk."

"Really?" she says, but I note a faint smile through the tears.

"Sure. If you cry, the uh, Spilled Milk Police will come and get you. We'd better hurry."

She pats the milk on the table while I scoop up the floor towels. We're done in no time.

"See, all better."

We go back to eating our breakfast. Before long, Dad comes downstairs. "Everything good here?" Em and I look at each other.

"Emma poured her own cereal and milk this morning," I say.

"That's wonderful." Dad spies the towels. "Oh. Don't worry. You'll get better each time you try." He scoops the wet paper towels off the table and dumps them in the garbage. "Change is good. Like the two of you; you're getting so mature. You're both growing up so fast, sometimes I hardly recognize you."

Emma drops her spoon. She reaches for her neck,

the same movement I've seen a million times, except she has no Beenie to grab hold of this time. She takes a few shallow breaths and the tears flow again. "Oh, honey." Dad rushes over to hug her.

She wipes her eyes. "I shouldn't cry. The Spilled Milk Police will come and get me."

Dad stares right at me.

"No, you're fine," I say. "You're not crying over spilled milk. You're crying over – "

I'm about to say "Beenie" until I realize no, that's not who she's crying about. My sentence hangs in the air, unfinished. And it will stay there. I'm not going to be the one to bring up Mom if no one else will.

CHAPTER TWENTY-SIX

At school, I move as quickly as possible when I reach my locker. Unfortunately, Brandon and Nick have no trouble sneaking up on me. Again.

They startle me when I turn around. Brandon grins menacingly. Sensing bloodshed, a crowd has already gathered. I attempt to remain calm. "Hi, Brandon. Did you have a nice weekend?"

"Yeah." He smacks his fist against his hand. "I spent my weekend thinking about all the ways I was going to pound you."

"Oh. I hope you did other things, too. No offense but that sounds like a boring weekend."

His grin fades. "Huh? I did other things."

"Like what?"

"Like, I don't know, my grandmother came over."

"Cool, so did mine. She cooked us dinner and gave us snacks. No big surprise - love and food are basically the same to her. Maybe that's just a Chinese thing."

"Nah, mine's like that -"

"He's doing it again," Nick says. "He's trying to distract you."

Once Nick reminds Brandon that he's supposed to hate me, he scowls and grabs my shirt.

I squirm beside his massive fist. "All I'm doing is talking to you like a person, which is more than Nick can say."

Brandon looks at Nick and back to me. For an instant, I think reason might prevail, but his anger wins out. Can't say I blame him. I know all about how anger can cloud your judgment. Watching it unfold before me is no less disturbing than experiencing it for myself.

"Nick's right," Brandon says. He yanks me so close, I can smell his cavities. "You're trying to trick me. Well, you're not getting out of it this time, you little weasel."

Brandon levels his fist with my face. "Hold up, did you just call me a weasel?"

"Yeah."

"No, I don't think so."

"What? Yeah, you are. You're a weasel." A weasel. Can you believe this guy?

"I am definitely not. Weasels are bold carnivores, extremely aggressive when their territory is invaded. They eat up to forty percent of their body weight every day, and they kill their prey by biting its neck or crushing its skull with sharp canines. I want you to think about this. Does that really sound like me?"

"Not...really, no."

"So 'weasel' doesn't work."

He lowers his fist. "I guess not."

Nick shrieks. I think his head might pop off. "Stop talking already and hit him!"

Brandon looks sideways at Nick. In the momentary silence that follows, a rhythmic clanging rings down the hallway. Brandon releases my shirt. The crowd scatters. "Everything OK here, boys?"

"Yes, Mrs. Vespa," we say.

"Brandon, shouldn't you be in homeroom?"

He takes a step back. "Jake and I were just talking."

"I see. Remember, when you talk to your classmates, you must always keep your hands to yourself."

"Yes, Mrs. Vespa."

Phew. Saved by the wrist chimes. Now all I have to do is avoid Brandon for the next ten mods and maybe I can delay my execution another day.

"See ya later, Jake," Brandon says. He smiles in the manner of a crocodile. "In gym class."

Oh, right. Today's an A day. So much for that bright idea.

CHAPTER TWENTY-SEVEN

"Hey," Aiden says when I walk into homeroom. He's standing by the doorway and holding a stack of index cards.

"Hey," I say back. "You all set?"

He flicks his thumb against the corner of his index cards. "This is going to suck."

"I'm sure it'll be fine."

"No, seriously. My group's a mess. I don't blame you for bailing, though. Hey, sorry about bringing up your mom. That wasn't cool. I was mad, you know, I didn't mean anything by it."

"Oh," I say. "It's all right."

"No, it isn't. I know better. And what I said about you?" He cringes. "It's not like I was fun to be around after my parents got divorced, and you stayed friends with me. I should have tried harder after your mom died. I don't even remember why we stopped hanging out."

"Like you said, I got all moody after she died."

His head droops. "I already said I was sorry."

"Yeah, but you weren't totally wrong. I do get moody sometimes. I can't always, you know, I can't always help it."

"That's all right." Aiden slaps my arm. "Oh, you were right about Will. He's a bit odd, but he's OK. I don't know why I ever listened to Nick."

We nod at each other. That's the one thing we always agree on, the one thing that still binds us together, our one shared truth: don't ever be like Nick.

He goes back to his index cards, and I notice Jess across the room.

"Hey," I say after walking over to her.

"Hey yourself. Sorry about what happened this weekend. I didn't mean to – I don't want you to get the wrong idea."

I try not to look crushed.

"I know you'll be great today," she says. "I didn't mean to imply that you weren't taking the project seriously. I don't know anyone who knows more about animals than you do. I mean, you were the first person I thought to ask. I'm glad you're in my group."

"Um. Wait, so that's the thing you don't want me to get the wrong idea about?"

She sighs and flashes the cutest smile.

Yeah, now I'm totally confused. Forget the manual, girls should come with subtitles.

"Too bad you don't know as much about people as you do about animals," she says.

"Animals are better."

"Why?"

"They never let you down."

She stares right through me. I don't know why I shared that with her. For a moment I feel exposed, as in one of those dreams where I stand before a crowd while dressed only in my underwear. You know the one.

"I'm just joking around," I say, hopeful she'll let it slide.

"Sure," she says. "I know."

CHAPTER TWENTY-EIGHT

After the first bell, Mrs. Vespa informs us that we'll present our projects in the same order she handed them out. Norman pops out of his chair at the front. Two girls from the back row walk forward. The head popular girl drops a note on my desk when she passes. I swat the thing and glance over to see if Mrs. Vespa noticed. When the coast is clear, I slide the note toward me until it falls on my lap. I open it under my desk. The note is written in a frilly scrawl and arranged like a bad poem:

> he did an outline not the whole thing
>
> but your idea was still good
>
> thanx Brandi

She dotted the *i* at the end of her name with a heart. Using a red felt-tip pen. The rest of the note is in black ink, so this means she must carry around a red felt-tip pen just so she can draw a tiny heart when she writes her name. Crazy.

Norman's topic is the elephant ivory trade. Their presentation is pretty gruesome. When they get to the part about how the poachers rip into the elephant to dig out the tusks, I get Jess' attention and make a vomiting gesture. She mouths the words "I'm OK" and smiles, filling my body with a warmth so powerful I have to look away.

I'll bet she'd never draw a goofy heart over the *i* in her name.

Aiden's group goes next. He wasn't kidding – their presentation is a mess. They discuss the death of coral reefs around the world. Aiden does OK, but his partners read from their slides with zero emotion. I doubt I'm the only one who drifts off.

We're up next. As planned, Jess opens, Will sets, and I spike. By the time we're through, the class is rapt with the plight of orangutans. Everyone is ready to charter a plane and fight beside our orange brethren. Well, everyone except for one.

"I don't get why we should care," Nick says. "I've never even heard of Sumatra. What country is that in?"

Mrs. Vespa gestures for me to answer.

Crud. I should probably know this. While I wrack my brain, Norman writes furiously on a piece of paper. He holds up the page so I can see it. Oh, no way.

"Indonesia," I say or, rather, read.

"That's correct."

Norman puts the paper down and dips his head. I guess Brandi shared our little secret with him. Like with my helping him, Norman makes no move to take credit. Well played.

"Yeah, whatever," Nick says. "I've never heard of that place either. And I still don't get why we should care. I mean, how does this affect *us*? Why should I be against palm oil if it's used in all those different things? I mean, if palm oil is so useful, why shouldn't we make more of it? If the choice is between helping people and helping orangutans, I say we help people."

"Interesting take," Mrs. Vespa says, "but beyond the scope of the presentation."

"Actually, I'd like to answer his question," I say. "I think Nick brings up an important point."

The class murmurs. Mrs. Vespa's bracelets jingle. Jess shoots me a look, and Will stifles a chuckle. As usual, Will has figured me out.

"All right," Mrs. Vespa says. "Go ahead."

"Like Nick, corporations will often state environmental problems like we have to choose between the needs of animals and the needs of people, but that's not usually true and it's definitely not true in this case. The people who live on Sumatra rely on the same forest for food, water, clothing, and shelter. The destruction of the forest causes them to lose their homes as well as their livelihood. They either have to move to the congested cities or stay and work the palm oil plantations where they are exploited and barely earn enough to survive.

"Unsustainable palm oil causes the destruction of both the human and animal communities. The corporations make a profit, but the entire world suffers from climate change, pollution, and the ultimate extinction of many important species. This affects all of us, even those of us who don't like to look at maps. And orangutans aren't the only animals affected. I can go into more detail on the tigers, rhinos, and elephants suffering the same fate."

"That won't be necessary," Mrs. Vespa says. This is a relief since I'm totally bluffing. "Thank you, Jessica, Will, and Jake. Excellent presentation."

Jess beams. Will and I bump fists. When I sit down, I see Nick scowling at me. I smile back.

"Good question, Nick. Thanks."

"I can't wait 'til gym when I get to watch Brandon finally beat that smug look off your face."

"Well," I say, "it's important to have goals."

CHAPTER TWENTY-NINE

Since today's Monday, I must stop by my locker to grab my gym bag. Every weekend we have to bring home our stinky gym clothes and wash them. I'm super jittery at my locker, but I manage to retrieve my bag without a run-in with Brandon.

Not that it matters; I see him soon enough. He's right ahead of me in the hallway going the same place I am: the gym locker room. If you're ever interested in getting beat up in your underwear, the gym locker room is definitely the place to go. I can almost taste Brandon's knuckles crushing my teeth.

The thought makes me dizzy. I've tried to be all cool about it, but now that I'm almost there, I shuffle along, each step closer to my execution. My panic must cause me to hallucinate because I think I see Mr. C. standing outside the gym and greeting the students as they pass. I don't remember him ever doing this before. When I approach, he blocks my path with his hand.

"Jake. Come with me."

Seriously, can this day get any worse? I follow him to his office. He motions for me to sit.

"I've heard the problem you and Brandon had at gym class last week may not be settled."

"You'll have to ask Brandon about that."

"I'm asking you."

"Well it's, I mean, it's settled as far as I'm concerned."

"So there's no risk that you'll start a fight today?" That *I'll* start a fight today? His mustache must be growing into his brain. He cannot possibly be serious.

"With Brandon? I'm going to start a fight with Brandon? With a kid who's twice my size?"

Mr. C. shrugs as if the size difference hadn't occurred to him. "I'm just making sure. Mrs. Vespa mentioned that there might be a problem with you and Brandon at gym class today."

"Right. So you thought *I* might start a fight with *him?*"

"No one's blaming either party here. I simply want to make sure nothing happens in the locker room. You can think about that while you get changed." He points to my bag. "I'll be waiting outside." This is ridiculous. I pull out my gym clothes and strip down to my underwear and socks. Why would Mr. C. drag me in here? Why not drag in Brandon? Wouldn't that make more sense? Actually, no, that's a terrible idea. If Mr. C. brought him in here, Brandon would be furious. He'd probably race right out of this office and pound me before I even had the chance to calm him down. Good thing Mr. C. completely messed that up.

Wait a second. It occurs to me, as I dump my regular clothes into my bag, that he and Mrs. Vespa may have a better understanding of the situation than I thought. Passing Mr. C. on my way to the gym, I mumble a thanks. He takes my bag and says nothing.

CHAPTER THIRTY

Mr. C. divides us into four teams for a volleyball tournament. Will's on my team, so we win the first game easily. Like I said before, the guy's a ringer. Unfortunately, this means we have to face Nick and Brandon's team for the championship. I avoid eye contact, but their loathing seeps through the net.

I need to think up a way to end this problem before things get completely out of hand. I've had success in pushing it off, but that hasn't really solved anything. Even if I make it through gym today, even if I make it all the way to the buses unscathed, there'll still be tomorrow and the day after that and the day after that. There's no point in delaying this any longer. Like when I avoid the basement in my dreams, I'm just prolonging the agony.

So how do I survive this? I wonder if my dreams can help me out, but I'm pretty sure this bully won't be defeated by hand puns. I think about what Dad said, how you can't always see the solution by looking directly at the problem. I decide to look a little bit off to the side.

Then it hits me. And by *it* I mean the volleyball, travelling at a terrific speed right into my skull. The force of impact lands me on my butt. Gasps are followed by silence except for the slap of the volleyball against the gym floor. Brandon stands by the net with a cocky grin plastered across his mug.

If I were in a cartoon, birds would be flying in a tight circle over my head right about now, or maybe I'd stagger about asking people where I was or something, but I experience none of this. I feel pretty good besides the burning pain in my forehead. For once, I have absolute clarity. My gut instinct shifts into fight-or-flight mode: attack him or run away in tears.

Both are terrible ideas. Thankfully, I have experience with ignoring my gut instinct. I know what I have to do. I leap to my feet and step over to where Will has picked up the ball.

"I'll take that."

He hesitates. "Are you sure?"

"Give me the ball." He hands me the ball as though it's a bomb set to explode. If he's right, we will find out soon enough. I stoop under the net and head straight towards Brandon.

Everyone on the other team takes two steps back except for Brandon. When he shifts to face me, his smirk has been replaced by a puzzled expression that seems to say *this is nothing like you.*

He's right, and that's the point. I had beaten my

dream bully only when I played by his rules. Here I go again.

Brandon looks at me, at the ball clenched in my hands, and me again. He shifts in place.

I mask my true emotions with a playful smile. "I knew you'd think up a way to get even. You nailed me good." I grin ear to ear, as though getting beaned in the head was the greatest thing ever to happen to me.

Brandon relaxes. His bafflement gives way to a belly laugh. We share a weird moment, like we're buddies enjoying a private joke. I toss him the ball and stoop under the net. Behind me, I hear Nick's agitated voice.

"Wait, so that's it?"

"Yep," Brandon says. "I got him back. We're even now."

"But you're supposed to fight him."

"Now I don't need to. I nailed him good."

"But...but you said you'd fight him."

"No, I said I'd get him back. Quit trying to tell me what to do all the time."

I turn around just in time to see Brandon shove Nick.

Mr. C. blows his whistle. "OK, people. Let's get back to the game."

The students rotate into position. I notice Mr. C. staring at me. He wiggles his mustache. I'm not sure what this means, but it's probably the closest thing to approval I've ever gotten from a gym teacher.

We head to the locker room after the game. On the way, Mr. C. hands me my bag. He doesn't say a word and neither do I. That was pretty cool of him. I vow never to make fun of his mustache again.

Actually, *never* is a really long time. Let's just say for a week. Definitely for the rest of today. Yeah, that's doable. I will not make fun of his goofy mustache for the rest of the day, no matter what. Unless he takes out his mustache comb. That's fair. The mustache comb doesn't count. That thing is ridiculous.

Will jogs up to me and pats me on the back. "That was awesome. I knew you'd figure out a way to solve the problem."

I nod. He actually did call it. "Although the next time a volleyball comes flying at your head," he says. "You should duck like a duck."

"Good one."

Inside the locker room, Brandon ignores me. In fact, I don't see him again until after mod ten when we happen to walk past each other in the hallway. He chuckles as if reliving the funny time he smacked my skull with a volleyball and knocked me on my butt. But it's not a mean chuckle. I'm in on the joke.

CHAPTER THIRTY-ONE

At the end of the day, I find Nick standing by my locker with his arms crossed. Even without Brandon by his side, Nick spikes my anger just by being there. "You again? Aren't we done with this already?"

"Yeah, yeah," he says. "You showed me up. As usual."

Hold up. He's mad at me?

"That's on you," I say. "I wouldn't ever have to show you up if you'd just leave me alone."

While Nick glowers at me, I remember something Mom used to say.

Whenever you're having a problem with somebody, take a moment to see things from the other person's point of view. A little empathy will go a long way. Everyone has good and bad inside, and most people are pretty decent once you get to know them.

Maybe she's right, but I can't see Nick's side to this at all.

"What's your problem with me anyway?" I say. "We used to get along. We used to be friends. Did I, like, do something to you I don't know about?"

"Oh, of course not. The great Jake? Why would he ever do anything wrong? He's perfect. My mom always says what a good boy that Jake is. Why can't you be more like Jake? Such a fine boy. If only you could be more like Jake. I am so sick of *Jake!*" I watch him seethe. Nick hasn't been this genuine with me in years. I actually remember what it was like to be friends.

"Wow. Sorry, man. That blows. But, you know, that doesn't really have anything to do with me. I mean, this sounds more like a problem between you and your mother."

His cheeks flush a fiery red. "Don't you dare talk about my mother. You don't get to – what do you know about mothers anyway? Yours is dead."

My whole body tightens. "Yeah, real mature," I say. I try to sound all chill, but my voice cracks.

"What's the matter? You gonna cry?"

I want to say no, but I can't get my words out. Nick has replaced his scowl with a wicked grin. He's thrilled that he's hurt me, but he hasn't really, at least not in the way he thinks. I know my mother died – that's not news – it's that I miss her. I miss her so much I can't breathe.

Just as I'm about break down, I remember something else Mom used to say. The last bit after that whole empathy thing.

Showing empathy will work for most people but not for everybody. Some people are just jerks.

When I remember the last part, I burst out laughing. That's Nick in a nutshell: a jerk. Mom nailed it.

Nick's face goes sour again. He storms away, cussing me under his breath. I guess he's disappointed he couldn't make me cry. Not this time, anyway. I'm sure he'll have plenty more opportunities to try again. Oddly enough, I'm not as worried about that as I would have been just a week ago. It's good to have friends again. "What's his deal?"

I spin around to face Jess.

"I don't know. Guess he's upset I didn't get beat up in gym."

"Oh, yeah. I heard Brandon nailed you with a volleyball."

"Yep."

"How'd you pull that off?"

I shrug. "Who knew not paying attention would come in handy? If only that worked in all my classes."

Jess smiles. "You know, I was thinking. Now that you know how to get to my house, maybe you can come over this weekend."

"Sure. That'd be fun. Um, do you think your mom would be all right with that?"

"Yeah, she still likes you." Jess leans closer and whispers, "But next time we have to remember to close the door."

She winks as she leaves. My mouth hangs open. For the second time in as many minutes, I'm speechless. But this time, in a wonderful way.

CHAPTER THIRTY-TWO

At dinner, I'm all set to tell the story of my science presentation, but I never get the chance. Emma's all mopey about her missing Beenie, and Dad's irritable about who knows what, so dinner is super awkward. I'm used to them trying to cheer me up, not the other way around. I find myself unsettled in a way that even a few hundred attempts at Orb Quash before bed can't fix.

After I climb under my covers, my thoughts drift to Mom. I wish I could tell her everything. I mean, I almost kissed a girl and now she wants me to come over again. It makes me nervous, but it's a good nervous, a happy nervous.

Getting all toasty under the covers reminds me of sunshine on the hot sand. That was many years ago, the last time we all went to the beach.

During Mom's last healthy summer, a few weeks

before her diagnosis, we drive out to Ocean City. We plant our umbrella in the sand near the carnival rides at the spot we had picked when riding the Ferris wheel. I jump the waves with Dad while Mom digs holes with Emma. When Dad and I return to the towels, Emma shows us all the stuff she's collected. Her take is mostly trash and broken seashells but she finds one object that interests me. It's frosted white and impossibly smooth.

That's sea glass, Mom says. I want it, but now that it has a name, Emma won't let me have it. I decide to search for my own piece, digging one hole after another. Mom keeps telling me how rare it is, how hard it is to find, not realizing this just makes me want it more.

I've got it, I say.

You found a piece?

No, I've got an idea. We'll walk up the shoreline.

Mom squints up the strip of land. The beach extends into the horizon. *How far?*

Until we find it, I say.

After a bit of negotiation, we compromise on the distance to the kite shop. I figure I get the better end of that deal, but after an hour or so, the kites loom closer and I have nothing to show for it. Looking for sea glass is hard work, let me tell you. Before long, the beach is crowded with people flying kites and me digging furiously.

Mom stuffs her phone in her pocket and tells me Dad and Emma will meet us up here. I dig faster. I figure when Dad arrives, that ends my treasure hunt.

We'll take a break for dinner, Mom says.

I'm not hungry. I am, in fact, starving but too engrossed to care.

Before long, Dad calls out from the boardwalk. Mom tells me to keep at it and walks over to him. I keep at it.

When Mom comes back, she suggests a spot for me to dig. Sure enough, I find it. My sea glass is smoky green, even more amazing than Emma's. I hold the thing straight through dinner, eating the entire meal with my other hand. Mom and I smile at each other. I know she thinks she's pulled one over on me, but I know better. You see, I had searched that exact spot she suggested before she came over. I know she put the sea glass there for me to find.

I don't remember much about the rest of the trip, just that walking around with my family and my sea glass, I'd never felt so safe and loved.

When we get home, I place the sea glass on my desk. I imagine it has special powers. Whenever I want, I can grip the glass in my fist and pull out the sunshine from that day. I hold it quite a few times after Mom gets sick. It keeps me from worrying so much. I know if Mom could find a way to the sea glass, she can find a way to get better.

The first time she goes into the hospital, I go to work drawing her a picture of the sea glass. I spend hours on it until I reproduce the magic with colored pencils. She tells me it's her favorite drawing. She brings it to her visits with the doctors, sandwiched in a folder among her medical reports and her lists of questions. She posts the drawing over her hospital bed whenever she has to stay overnight. It's always near her, including when she dies.

The glass was a fraud, of course. It never had any special powers - just a lump of polished trash that looked pretty, just another lie in a world littered with lies.

One of the first things I did after Mom died was

throw away my sea glass. I dropped it right in the garbage. Plunk. Gone forever.

I have to admit, though. Some nights, like tonight, I really wish I hadn't done that.

CHAPTER THIRTY-THREE

When the fuzzy dream world emerges, I waste no time. I pull the world into sharp focus and push the air with both hands. I'm in an empty room with the dream on a screen before me like at the end of my last dream. Time to conjure up my plan.

CONNOR.

The kangaroo appears. His gaze darts around the room. Before Connor can get his bearings, I think my next word.

BAZOOKAPUS.

The furry green monster appears, white eyebrows ablaze.

"Hey, buddy. I got you a snack." I point at Connor. The bazookapus scarfs him down in one gulp and wags his tail furiously. I scratch him under his ears.

"Good boy. Did it taste good?"

The bazookapus tents his eyebrows. "Not really my cup of tea, old bean." He runs his tongue across his teeth. "Sort of a yeasty tang like Vegemite. Well, I must be off. Cheerio."

He nuzzles against my face and thunders into the distance. A portal opens by the screen. Connor hops toward me, muck dripping from his ears. When he shakes, brown spittle flies off his fur.

He sniffs the spittle. "That mystery's solved. Those things eat chocolate."

"And he drinks tea."

"Well he is from Buckinghamshire originally." Connor picks goopy chocolate wads off his fur and flicks them away. "You didn't really think you could get rid of me so easily?"

I shrug. "Worth a shot."

"Listen, mate. No more goofing around. Come to the basement."

I had wanted to go, but the moment he says "basement," I panic.

"No. I can't deal with that right now."

"Right now? You never want to deal with it. That's your problem. You fight it, you use anger to mask your sadness, you bury your emotions, hoping that will make it all go away, but it doesn't go away. It comes here, deep within you, into my world. The only way to be rid of it is to face it. Jake, come to the basement now."

For a moment, we're in front of the basement door, but I pull us back.

CANNON.

While closing one eye, I squeeze Connor's image

down to cannonball size. I toss him into the cannon's muzzle and yank the string. He blasts out, streaking across the sky. I watch him shrink into a speck before exploding into multicolored fireworks. The lights sparkle in the distance, but I know. I know.

"You're standing behind me, aren't you?"

"If you think I'm standing behind you, then I'm standing behind you." Sure enough, Connor stands behind me, his hair singed but otherwise no worse for wear.

"So I can't get rid of you?"

"Of course not. I'm your greatest nemesis, remember." He winks. "I think it's time for you to come to terms with who I really am."

Yeah, my greatest nemesis, whoever that is. "Are you supposed to be Nick?"

The kangaroo laughs. "Nick? He's just a jerk, remember. You'll meet all sorts of jerks in life. They're not important. No, Jake. Who is the person most responsible for your problems? Who is the one person you need to get past before you can do anything?"

"I don't know," I say.

"You *do* know. If I know, then you know. And if you know, then I know."

"Can you please stop speaking in riddles?"

"We can be very frustrating, can't we?" We? He can't mean the two of us.

"You're nothing like me."

"I'm not?" The kangaroo shape-shifts into my clone. It's like staring into a mirror except my reflection creeps toward me out of my control.

"Stop it."

"Stop what?" my reflection says. "This is what we look like."

"You're not me."

"Who else could I possibly be? Who else do you need to get past before you can do anything? You, Jake. Your greatest challenge is yourself."

"That's...it can't be true."

"Really? Who pushed his friends away? Who keeps things from his family? You, Jake. It's always you. You focus on jerks and bullies, but the person you need to work on is yourself."

I refuse to believe him. Yet, the more I think about it, the more I realize the truth in what he said. I do push people away before they can get too close. I do keep things from my family. And since these are my dreams, I must be creating all this. In the form of a kangaroo, no less. As absurd as it sounds, it does explain everything. Well, except for one thing.

"You can't be me. I wouldn't want to hurt myself."

"Hurt you? No, Jake. I've been trying to help you. But you keep fighting me. Fighting yourself as usual. You're so conflicted, you've found a way to enter your own dreams just to battle yourself some more. This isn't healthy. You need to stop."

"That can't be right. Why would I create the turtles?"

"You put them here to punish yourself. They guard the route to Mom. They are your fear, your anger. Only you can get rid of them. And please do. They're extremely annoying."

"Wait, you don't like the turtles either?"

"Of course not. They're repulsive. They smell like old

socks. And the big, ugly one cheats at backgammon."

"Hold up. You *play* with the turtles?"

Connor is a kangaroo again. He rests back on his tail and crosses his arms. "Sure. We've got to have something to do while you're awake. It's not like we have electronics around here."

"But it's the dream world. Can't you – forget it, I'm overthinking this. Tell me what I need to do."

"You already know what you need to do. Are you ready for the basement?"

I take a deep breath. It's quite refreshing. The actual me must have taken a deep breath at the same time.

"Let's go."

Before I finish my sentence, we're already there. Connor knocks on the basement door. I hear heavy thumps closing in. "How exactly does he cheat at backgammon?"

"Whenever he's losing, he drools on the board," Conner says. "The pieces get so nasty, it's just – blah."

The door swings open revealing a sea green creature with a pointed shell on his back and beady eyes. He towers over me. "What do you want?"

"I want you to leave."

He turns to the two giant turtles behind him. They snicker and howl.

"Do you, now? And who's going to make us?"

"I am. I don't know why I ever put you here, but I'm taking you away now. I don't want you here any longer. Go."

They respond with deep turtle laughter. It sounds splashy, like castaways thrashing in a vast ocean. The turtles crowd closer.

Why did I think telling them to leave would work?

Oh well. I suppose I could wake myself up, but why bother? They'd just be back, night after night, over and over and over again. So what if they trample me. They block the path to Mom. I will not give up.

And really, how scary can he be if he has to cheat at backgammon?

"Do you really cheat at backgammon?"

The turtle laughter ceases.

"Who told you that?" The big, ugly one blinks at me. "I never cheat."

"Except when you're losing," says the turtle behind him.

"What!"

"You always drool."

"I have a dental problem."

"Only when you're losing?"

Their argument becomes heated. They snap their jaws and bang their shells into each other.

"Enough of this," I say. "You're in my way. I don't want you here any longer." I rush down the stairs, bracing myself for impact, but it never happens. The images fade into mist. I find myself in the basement, unharmed.

I haven't been down here in years. And not just in my dreams. I haven't been in my actual basement for as long as I can remember. I walk to the only door.

"She must be in here."

"Wait, Jake." Conner hops by the door. His kangaroo ears are raised. "Are you sure you're ready?"

Ready? I've wanted this for years. I couldn't possibly be more ready.

"I finally got through."

"But are you sure you're ready?" Connor thumps his foot. "Just because you can doesn't mean you should."

"No more riddles. I'm tired of your games. I can enter my dreams. I can do anything."

"That still doesn't mean you should. I'll fight you again if I have to."

"And you think you'll win?"

"No. I think we'll lose."

This is not a threat I take lightly; I know what a pain I can be. But I don't care. The turtles are gone. I'm free to do whatever I want. I'm free to come back as many times as I want. I'll zone through each dull day and live for my nights. Who needs reality with all its problems? I've mastered my dreams. This will be epic.

My hands tremble with excitement. I touch the doorknob.

The colors shimmer. A restfulness flows through me, and my bedroom drifts into view: my alarm, my desk, my window. The lighting is early morning, dreary reality.

No. That can't be. The dream can't end, not after all that I've been through. I pound my fists against the mattress. As certain as I had been a moment ago that I had mastered my dreams, I realize now that I haven't and never will. I had a real opportunity to see Mom, and I blew it. My conceit did me in. This might have been my last chance.

Unless.

I reach for my nightstand and turn off my alarm. No safety for me. I'm going rogue.

CHAPTER THIRTY-FOUR

I've never once succeeded in returning to a dream after I wake up, but I must try. I clear my mind. Serenity seeps in, blurring the edges. My singular desire focuses me in a way I've never experienced before. A nothingness stretches before me. I don't react. It will happen when it happens.

The basement flickers into view. I seize control and the colors sharpen. But it seems...different, like a movie set after the filming is over. The cement walls are flimsy, held together by rope and duct tape, balanced at strange angles. Stage lights and cameras are stacked against the back. Men in overalls linger nearby, hunched over, murmuring.

Connor sits at a table in the center of the room. I hardly recognize him. He's no longer a kangaroo; he's a person in a kangaroo costume holding a kangaroo head under his arm. He kinda looks like me but older, with stubble and unkempt hair. Is this supposed to be future me? Do I become a hippie or something?

Next to him, a man wearing an orangutan costume sets his cards down. He waves and lifts his orangutan head off his lap. The head I recognize, but this other Owen is a man. He's pretty old too, easily thirty.

A woman turns around. She resembles Ginny except more mature and less boxy. Her hair is frizzy, and a sleek black bodysuit accentuates her curves. She smiles and points to a GPS device on the table. It's like I wandered into one of those trailers backstage at Disneyland. These guys completely weird me out.

Connor leaves the kangaroo head on the table and walks over. "I'm not even going to ask how you got back here."

That's good because I have no idea. "I came to see Mom. I have to go in."

"In?" He follows my gaze to the door. "Ah. If that's what you came for, then go ahead. No one is going to stop you. We're off the clock."

I grunt as if I'm listening, but really, I'm staring at Ginny. She's very distracting.

"Care to join us?" she says.

"What are you playing? Wait, no, I haven't come for that." I focus on the door, but my mind wobbles. Instead, I think about the turtles.

"No turtles," Connor says. "You moved past them, remember? No one can stop you, but no one will help you either. If you want to try again, you're on your own."

"Got it. Hey, thanks for everything. I understand now what you've been doing. That you've been trying to help.

And don't worry – I won't be back. I mean, obviously I will, but not as me. Once I do this, I'll never try to control my dream-self again."

Connor tilts his head. He narrows his eyes. I know he can see into my mind because that's where he lives, but I'm not worried. I mean what I say. That nonsense I thought earlier about living my life in my dreams told me all I need to know. The lure of fantasy could have destroyed me. I will do what I came here to do and then live my life in the real world, however dreary or painful.

A sad smile curves his lips. "Good. Good for you. That's the right call. I know what this means to you, what you're giving up." His gaze shifts to the back of the room. He bends down until his lips brush my ear and he whispers, "Don't touch the doorknob."

The cameramen abruptly stop murmuring. They glare at Connor, who walks back to the table. He picks up his cards as though nothing is wrong, but something is wrong. The men inch toward us from all directions, menacing, arching their backs. They move slowly like turtles. Connor peers from behind his cards.

"You don't have much time."

Men swarm around the walls. I race over to the door and reach for the knob, but I stop myself. Is this a trick? No, Connor's right. The basement isn't real, and Mom is not behind the door. If I touch the handle, the door will open to nothing, and I will wake up again.

I have no idea what to do next. The men crowd around me, their hot breath prickling my skin, but I do not acknowledge them, so they cannot touch me.

This door must be a portal, but how can I get

through it? I realize I can't, at least not by myself. I brush my fingertips against the door. A warm mist flows over my hand. I recognize the sensation, one I haven't experienced in years. Mom. She is in here, but not in this room. She's in my head.

Take me to wherever you are. I need to see you, Mom.

I relax and allow the dream to take over. The room swirls. I am no longer in control.

CHAPTER THIRTY-FIVE

I find myself in a room containing a hospital bed. A woman lies under the covers, her head angled away. Wires and tubes connect her to beeping machines and dripping bags of fluid. My childhood nightmare, as requested. Buried memories overwhelm me. I watch my dream-self walk closer until I'm beside her. The sterile white walls envelop us. I see no door, no way in or out.

Mom turns her head. Despite the hospital setting, she looks great. Healthy Mom, before she lost her hair. Before we went shopping for wigs. Before she said "How about this one? How about this one?" as though we were picking out fruit instead of a cover for her bald head to better pretend she wasn't dying.

The moment takes my breath away.

"I've been waiting for you." She frowns. "You look

blurry. Jake, you're dreaming."

The moment she tells me I'm dreaming, the colors sharpen. I regain control of my body.

"Hi, Mom. I've missed you."

She grips my hand. Her familiar warmth settles me.

"You're so much older. My darling boy."

That was a cutesy nickname Mom used to call me. It really has been a while. I'm about to ask her not to call me that, but I figure it's not like anyone else can hear her, so whatever.

"How have you been?" I ask.

"I haven't been anything; I've been waiting. I need to know, Jake. How are you?"

How am I? "I haven't been doing so well."

"I see," she says. "The pain surrounds you. It's a blackness that swirls and throbs."

I scan the room but see nothing except the blinding whiteness. "How do I get rid of it?"

"You get rid of pain by sharing it with another person. Let me be that person. It's only fair since I'm the cause."

"The cause?" What the heck does she mean? "It's not like dying was your fault."

"Are you sure you believe that? It's important to be honest. You can only heal with the truth."

I flinch. "I'm not...I'm not angry with you. That's stupid. You didn't choose to die. Why would I be angry with you?"

"I don't know. Tell me." She folds her hands on her lap.

This is ridiculous. I'm angry at everyone else, sure,

but not her. All she did was die. All she did was leave me motherless. All she did was go away when I needed her most. OK, so I might be a little bit angry with her. The moment I think this, a fury I cannot suppress seizes me.

"Why did you have to leave us? Yes, I know, you got sick and died, but I wasn't ready. I wasn't ready for you to go. I feel like...like you abandoned us. Me, Emma, and Dad. And yeah, I know that's stupid. I know you didn't choose to die. It's not your fault. But it's still what happened. So yeah, I'm angry. But I can't be angry at you. That makes no sense. I try not to be angry. I try really hard." I clench my hands until my nails dig into my palms. "But it never works. I'm still angry."

"It's OK, Jake. You don't have to fight it." Her voice is reassuring, smooth like sea glass. "Feelings are never stupid. They don't have to be rational. They don't have to make any sense at all. They're how you feel. You can be angry with me if you need to be. I was angry, too. I was furious when the doctors diagnosed me. I can't die, I told them. I'm a mother with two small children. Then I let my anger ruin me more than the cancer ever could. I became a bitter wife and an absent mother. But when I finally realized how my anger affected my family, I knew I had to stop. I decided not to be angry anymore."

The machine by her bed beeps rhythmically, marking the passage of time.

"You can't just decide not to be angry," I say. "That's impossible."

"Impossible?" With a sweeping hand gesture, she calls attention to the room. "There is no impossible. You know this. You can choose to be any way you want. I managed to stop my anger by focusing on the good things instead: Emma's giggles, your father's adorable bumbling, that oh-so-serious look you get when you draw. Over time, I learned not to be so angry. I got better at it until I reached the point where I could enjoy what little time I had left. Each day was a blessing. I was lucky to have known you. You're lucky, too."

"I don't feel lucky."

"I understand. You got a raw deal. All children should be able to grow up with two parents. But many don't. It happens all the time, and it stinks. There's nothing I can say to make it better. All you can do is focus on the good things instead. For you, that's your father and sister, the two people who love you most."

My hands ball into fists again. Emma? Is she serious? And I don't even know about Dad anymore. "Dad and I don't talk much," I say. "He's too busy trying to replace you. He's probably off doing that right now."

"No, he's not. He's where he is every morning. Outside your room. Waiting for your alarm to go off so he can make sure you're OK. He will be there for you like always."

I don't believe her. How could she know that anyway? She can't know anything I don't know. She's just my imagination. She isn't real. Mom is dead.

The beeping gets faster, the pitch more shrill.

"Wait, what's happening?"

She's become ashen, haggard, like when I saw her for the last time.

"Don't worry, Jake." Her voice is hoarse. "I'm not in pain. This has already happened."

I shake the bed. "Stop. Don't do this."

"This is how you imagined it."

"But...I don't know. I wasn't there. I could be wrong."

Her breathing is shallow. Her body spasms.

"No! Dad said they turned off the machines in the end. That it was peaceful."

Her eyes flutter open. "But you don't believe him."

She's right. I always assumed Dad lied to make it sound better for Emma and me. And probably he did, but so what. Maybe it's time I give Dad a break. I decide not to be angry.

The machines fall silent. Mom wipes the sweat off her brow. "Thanks. I feel better now."

She looks better, too. Like before. Healthy Mom is back.

"Please don't do that again."

"I didn't do anything, Jake. You are the keeper of your memories. And you are the composer of your nightmares." She's right, of course. Sucks for me because I have a vivid imagination.

Mom shakes her head. "Don't be mad at your imagination. That's one of the many things I love about you." I remember her saying that, and it sets me off again.

"Even if I can calm myself down, the anger always comes back. Sometimes, out of nowhere, I remember you died, and I get so sad I can't stand it. I want to scream and tear things up."

"Jake."

She touches my hand. I can't get over how familiar it is. "We had eight wonderful years together," she says. "I wouldn't trade them for anything."

Eight years sounds like a long time, but it isn't really. It's only a portion of my life, and every year the portion gets smaller and more distant. One day, it might fade to nothing, and I'll have lost her forever.

"No," she says. "Never. I'll always be here. In your mind, in your heart...maybe haunting your dreams." She winks.

I laugh. She knows just what to say. That's one of the good things about her. I'll try to think about that the next time I get angry. "I'd like that," she says.

"You know, Mom, this whole reading my mind thing is kinda freaking me out."

She straightens her back against the pillow. "Moms can always read their children's minds. Not just in dreams."

"I don't even want to know if that's really true." We share a laugh.

"I'm glad you visited," she said. "You know you're protected in here. But with that privilege comes responsibility."

Her tone makes me shiver. "What kind of responsibility?"

"You'll have to wake yourself up. You need to be the one to end this dream."

"No." I recoil. "I can't. I can't do it." That would be like her dying all over again.

She folds her hands on her lap. I know what that means: We will wait until you do as I say. Fine, then we'll wait.

"I'm not doing it. You can't make me do it. Why are you torturing me?"

"No one is torturing you. You're doing all of this to

yourself."

Of course I am. Apparently, I do it all the time.

"It's time to move on. It's time to let go."

"Never." I grab her hand.

"Not of me, silly, of your pain, your anger. Focus instead on my love. It'll be there for you whenever you need it. Wherever you are. Forever."

"OK."

She smiles. Her love swirls through me, invigorates me, clears away the darkness. That's why I came. Time to finish what I started. "My darling boy," she says.

"Please don't call me that."

"My big boy?"

I groan. "Yeah, that's really not any better."

She squeezes my hand. "I love you, Jake."

"I love you too, Mom," I say, and I wake myself up.

CHAPTER THIRTY-SIX

Waking up can be abrupt and distressing, much like getting kicked in the face by a kangaroo, but not this time. I ease into it. The magic fades until I'm fully awake, bundled beneath my blanket. Outside, the birds chirp. The morning sun filters across my room. I sit up. Standing in the doorway, Dad stares at me. I can't say I'm surprised to see him. "I've never watched anyone express so many emotions in their sleep," he says. "If you ever want to let me in, I'd love to know what's going on in your head." I prop my pillow against the wall and scoot over to make room. Dad takes me up on the offer. The mattress creaks under his weight.

"Is it true that you stand outside my door every morning to make sure I get up OK?"

Dad hangs his head. "Busted."

"Wait, you really do that?"

"Usually I wait outside, but when you didn't get up at your regular time, I checked in on you. You looked so serious. Something told me not to wake you." A part of me wants to believe I know what the something is, but it can't be true. It was only a dream. Still, Mom had been right about Dad standing outside my room every morning.

"Thanks, I guess. You don't have to do that."

"Of course I don't have to. I want to. There's only the three of us. We need to look out for each other."

He may be looking out for me, but I haven't done much to look out for him. Or Emma. I really need to do better.

"I talked to Mom," I say, and I brace myself. Dad nods as if I hadn't said something crazy. "That doesn't surprise you?" I say. "That I was talking to Mom?"

"No, I talk to her too."

"Um, Mom's dead." I say this like I'm angry he didn't correct me, like I'm daring him to yell at me. Instead, he puts his arm around me. I'm getting a little old to be held. Well, I suppose I can let it slide this one time.

"I miss her," I say.

"I know. We all do."

"You do? No, you have those girlfriends. You're, like, lining up candidates to replace her."

I'm angry again. This is the opposite of what I want. I don't want him to stop holding me either, but I can't contain myself.

"No one can replace your mother."

"Then why do you –"

He cuts me off with a sigh. It's the saddest sigh I've ever heard. "Dads get lonely sometimes." His eyes glisten.

Great, now he's going to make me cry.

"Why would you get lonely? You've got me and Emma."

He laughs, but not in a mean way. "You're right. I do." He squeezes my shoulders. "You two keep me grounded. Without the two of you, I'd be lost."

I'm not sure what he means. How would he be lost? Doesn't matter. I like it when he talks to me as if I'm a grown-up. We haven't had a good talk in a while. The urge to tell him everything swells within me. "I finally took care of the turtles."

"The turtles?"

"In my dream. Three big, ugly turtles guard the basement where Mom is. They keep me from her. I've had this dream for years."

I have no idea how he'll react, but I would never have guessed what he says next.

"That makes sense."

I stare at him. "How could that possibly make sense?"

His confusion reflects my own. "You really don't remember? No, I guess you don't. I'll bet that's why you keep having the same dream."

I know he can tell that I don't understand. His lips tighten the way they often do when he is about to explain something.

"Your brain is trying to force you to confront a bad memory. You have to move past it before you can heal."

Yeah, I suppose that's why Conner kept dragging me back to the basement. I almost feel bad for blasting him out of a cannon.

"Your eighth birthday was a week after Mom died. We had planned a party for you – in the basement. We all assumed you'd want to cancel, but on the day of the party, when I tried to convince you to let me reschedule for another time, you flipped out. You said, 'I can't have my party just because Mom died?' We got into a huge argument."

I cringe. "Did I really say that?"

"Yes. Listen, everyone reacts differently to loss. You wanted to believe Mom's dying hadn't changed anything. I understood and, well, I gave in. I shouldn't have. I made the wrong call. Mom used to take care of this stuff. She would have known what to do, but I was overwhelmed. I focused on getting things ready. You know Mom. She purchased everything weeks in advance. I just had to find it all and set it up. You were into the Teenage Mutant Ninja Turtles back then."

"Oh yeah," I say.

"We had three huge posters of them. I put them up in the basement."

Dad and I nod at each other. I guess the dream wasn't as crazy as I thought.

"You paced around all afternoon, not knowing what to do with yourself. I was relieved when no one showed up. That was, at least, until you freaked out. I found Mom's list of your friend's phone numbers and called all the parents, but I could reach only two. They were both hesitant to come, so I begged them. 'Stop by. Don't worry about a gift.' The kids' moms tried to convince me to reschedule. 'Is he really ready to have a party?' they asked. You weren't, but I didn't know what else to do. I guilted them into coming over."

"What do you mean, you guilted them?"

Dad hangs his head. His embarrassment looks fresh, as if this had happened yesterday. "I said, 'Hey, my kid's mother just died. Are you seriously going to let him have a birthday party where no one shows up?' I just had to get someone to come over. This was yet another mistake. I was on a roll that day."

"I think I remember this, sort of. It's all pretty hazy."

"You and I never talked about it, but if you've been having nightmares, it has to come out. Fighting only makes it worse."

Connor had said that. And if Connor is me, I already knew.

"By the time Aiden and Jessica arrived with their moms, you'd calmed down a little, but you were still on edge. Your friends hadn't seen you in a week, since I took you out of school after Mom died. They weren't expecting you to be – you know, maybe we shouldn't talk about it."

"Tell me everything." The certainty in my voice surprises me. I really don't want to hear this, but I know I need to.

Dad rests his head against the wall. "OK. See, you wanted your friends there, but you couldn't deal with them. You were angry and rude, not at all your usual self. I realized it wasn't fair for your friends to see you like that. I told the moms they were right, that they just should go.

Aiden and his mom left but Jessica's mom wanted to stay and talk to you, so I took Jessica upstairs to watch TV. Jessica's mom came upstairs later to say you'd calmed down a bit and suggested we eat the cake."

"But you forgot to pick up the cake, right?"

"I don't remember if I even *ordered* the cake. I've

been making lists ever since. I hate forgetting things. Bad memories."

The lists. Of course.

"I apologized to Jessica on her way out, but she seemed unfazed. No big deal, just another disaster birthday party. She really impressed me. I'm glad you two are friends again. She's a great girl." Yeah, she is pretty great. "Unfortunately, things got bad again as soon as they left. You screamed, 'No one wanted to come, not even Mom.' I tried reasoning with you. I told you Mom wanted to be here more than anything. How hard she tried to stay well long enough to make it to your birthday. But you didn't understand. You said, 'No she didn't, or she would be here,' and you tore down the posters. After that, I left you alone."

"I remember," I say. "I remember tearing up the posters. And I remember feeling really guilty after. I picked out those posters when Mom took me shopping, before the last time she went into the hospital. Tearing up the posters, I felt like I was tearing her up. I was so mad at the time I didn't care but after, I felt terrible. I felt like...like it was my fault she died."

Dad hugs me. I can't hold back my tears any longer, but it's a good crying, like when you have a stomach flu and you finally throw up and all the nausea goes away. Let the bad come out. Mom used to say that when I was sick. I remember. I remember everything.

"There's one more thing you should know," Dad says. "After I left you alone to tear up the basement, I checked on Emma. I found her upstairs on her bed holding Beenie. Emma told me that now that Mom had gone away, Beenie would take care of her. That whenever she held Beenie, she could feel Mom hugging her back. I know Emma is too attached to that thing, but it makes her less scared. I can't believe she lost it."

"She didn't."

Dad stiffens. "Why do you say that?"

"Because Beenie's in my closet."

CHAPTER THIRTY-SEVEN

"What is Beenie doing in your closet?" His tone is more curious than harsh, but it makes me pause. No stopping now.

"I saw Beenie on the couch, and I thought about how Emma spends way too much time with that stupid thing, so I hid it."

Dad regards me suspiciously. "No, that's a cop-out. Try again."

"What? That's what happened."

He shakes his head, setting me off.

"What do you want me to say? That it makes me angry she's fine with Mom dying? That I can't understand why she never seems upset? That I took it because she loves that stupid monkey more than me?"

"Jake, no. Emma is like Mom. She tries to be

cheerful, but it's just a front. She's hurting as much as the rest of us. And Emma loves you more than you can imagine."

I don't know if he's trying to make me feel better, but all I feel is ashamed.

"I'm sorry I took Beenie. I didn't know Emma thought of her as Mom." I wipe my eyes. "Are you going to tell her what I did?"

"No," he says. "You are."

His stern expression wears me down.

"Fine. I'll tell her. Should we call her in?"

"In a moment. First I want to hear how you got past the turtles."

The turtles. I can't believe I was ever afraid of those jokers.

"Once I stopped being scared, they lost all their power over me. They didn't seem so menacing after I learned that the big, ugly one cheats at backgammon. I almost felt sorry for them."

"That's true with most bullies once you get to know them. You should remember that in case you meet up with a bully in real life."

Yeah, in case. I'm in middle school. That's like every day.

"Yes, I know. You're in middle school."

I gasp. "Wait, can you read my mind?"

"No, but I can read your expression. So, tell me, after you got past the turtles you saw Mom, right? How'd she look?"

"Good. Like before she got sick."

Dad smiles. "That's how I remember her, too." We're quiet for a moment. Thinking about Mom makes me angry, so I do what I promised and think about the good things. The anger fades, but a deep sadness fills the void.

"I wish people didn't have to die. Why can't everything stay the same?"

"I don't know if the question has an answer," Dad says. "All I know is things change all the time. Nothing lasts forever. Each phase of your life is followed by another until the end. The best you can do is enjoy what you have when you have it."

"Huh. Mom told me practically the same thing. She said to focus on the good things. I guess I must have heard you say it, so my brain had her say it."

Dad squirms. "Actually, I got that from her. I quote Mom all the time to you and Emma. But you're right – it was only a dream, only your memory of Mom. I'm sure it seemed real."

"It sure did. I learned a lot from Mom considering she was just my memory. She's the one who told me you wait outside my room every morning."

"Well, it's not like I've been subtle," he says. "Obviously a part of you must have figured it out."

"Yeah, the part of me that dresses up like a kangaroo."

Dad stares at me. "Should I know what that means?"

"No. Sorry. Mom told me other things. She said she was really angry when she first got sick and let her anger make everything worse until she learned to focus on the good things: Emma's giggles, my serious expression when I draw, and your, um, how did she put it? Oh yeah, your adorable bumbling."

His jaw hangs open. "How did you...that's

impossible."

"There is no impossible. Only a probable lack of imagination."

"I like that," Dad says. "Very witty. Still, you must have overheard her talking about my 'adorable bumbling.' When she was alive, I mean."

Not that I remember, but there's a lot I don't remember.

"If you say so. You probably won't believe this part either. Over the last week, when I'm dreaming, I realize I'm dreaming during the dream, and I can take control of my body."

"Seriously? You're a lucid dreamer?"

"I'm a...wait, that's a thing?"

"Sure. It's called lucid dreaming. Most people can't do it. In fact, most people don't believe it's even possible. I'd never met anyone who could until –"

He cuts himself off, but I know who he's talking about.

"Mom? Mom could do it? Cool, is this genetic?"

"I have no idea. She said she didn't do it often. I asked her why she didn't do it all the time, but she never really explained."

"I know why. It causes a mess of problems. I promised myself last night that I wouldn't do it anymore. Whenever I took control, I wound up fighting myself. It's not a situation either side can win. Things got pretty bad."

"So this is why you woke up screaming?"

I don't answer, but I don't really need to. Outside my room, the hallway creaks. "Sounds like Emma's awake," he says. "Are you ready to tell her?"

"I guess."

Dad shifts to the middle of the bed. "It'll be OK. You've often said you want to be a grown-up. What you're about to do is a grown-up thing."

"Hello?" Emma calls out.

"We're in here," Dad says.

"How is this a grown-up thing? Because I have to hurt someone?"

"No, Jake. Because you're going to do the right thing even though you don't want to."

Emma walks in, rubbing her eyes. "How are you, sweetheart?" Dad asks.

"I've got crusties."

"You go ahead and rub those out. Did you sleep OK?"

She sits down on the edge of my bed and sweeps the hair off her face. "Not really. I had weird dreams."

Dad shoots me a look. "Really."

"Me too, Em," I say. "What did you dream about?"

"Oh. I was out in the middle of the ocean in this rowboat. All these horrible noises were coming from below the water: screaming and fighting and stuff. It got me really scared. I looked around for Beenie, but I couldn't find her."

Great. Like I could possibly feel worse. I notice Dad staring at me, waiting.

"I know where Beenie is," I say.

Emma's face brightens. "Really?"

"Uh-huh. She's in my closet." Emma races over to the closet and opens the door. She searches frantically, waving her hands in the air. "Second shelf, under the towel."

She's so excited that she's freaking, but finally she

lifts the towel and finds Beenie. She hugs her monkey and dances around. The truth is going to crush her. And me.

"Thanks, Jake!"

"No. Don't thank me. I have to tell you something, Em. Stop spinning and listen. I was the one who took her."

She takes a stumble step. "You? You took her?"

"I saw Beenie on the couch, and I took her. I hid her in the closet. Two days ago." She twists her body and clasps her fingers around Beenie. Her eyebrows quiver. I've never seen her regard me with such venom.

"Why?"

When I gaze into her eyes, all my excuses wither to nothing. Why? I don't remember. Did I even have a reason? Yeah, all I thought about was myself. "I'm so sorry, Em. I didn't understand. I was being mean." Her expression causes me physical pain. I glance down at the carpet. "I'm a terrible brother."

She marches right toward me. I figure she's going to hit me, and I decide I'll let her. Go ahead, right in the face. I have it coming. Instead, she lays Beenie on my chest. "You can keep Beenie as long as you want." Emma positions her ridiculous monkey so it looks like Beenie's hugging me. "She'll make you feel better."

I wish Emma had hit me. It would have hurt less.

"That's very sweet," Dad says. "Jake, what do you say to your sister?"

I pluck Beenie off my chest. "I don't want to hug Beenie." Emma looks crushed. I put out my arms. "I want to hug *you.*"

She rushes over and leaps on me. She's soft and warm like Mom. She's my Beenie.

Dad cheers. The mattress springs creak when he bounces. He pulls us into his arms. Even Beenie's in on this. Dad holds Beenie in his hand and her monkey fur presses against my neck.

Family hug, I guess. All four of us, together again. I want the hug to last forever. But I know it won't, and I'm OK with that.

ACKNOWLEDEGMENTS

I would like to thank my parents for their encouragement and boundless confidence in me over these many years. I'm also grateful to Amy Betz for her insightful developmental editing and for always urging me to elevate the story. And big thanks to Cate Baum and the team at Kwill Books for their tireless work in guiding me over the final hurdles to bring Jake out into the world.

Thanks as always to Joyce Wong for her love and support and for sometimes laughing at my jokes (even when she tries hard not to) and to our children, Andrew and Sam, for sharing their lives and imparting youthful knowledge like how I just don't get this generation, and various other truisms.

ABOUT THE AUTHOR

After graduating from Wesleyan University, David J. Naiman obtained his medical degree at New York University School of Medicine and trained in the primary care internal medicine program at Johns Hopkins Bayview Medical Center. Writing nights and weekends, he published the award-winning #1 Amazon bestselling novel *Didn't Get Frazzled*, a work of humorous medical fiction for adults, under the pen name David Z Hirsch.

From there, David turned to children's literature to pursue the themes of family, friendship and the magic of childhood that continue to inspire him. *Jake, Lucid Dreamer* is his first middle grade novel. He lives in Maryland with his wife and two sons. Visit his website at www.davidjnaiman.com.

Made in the USA
Columbia, SC
19 January 2019